THE DAY I WAS
crucified

THE DAY I WAS
crucified

AS TOLD BY CHRIST HIMSELF

Gene Edwards

DESTINY IMAGE® PUBLISHERS, INC.
P.O. Box 310, Shippensburg, PA 17257-0310
"Promoting Inspired Lives."

This book and all other Destiny Image and Destiny Image Fiction books are available at Christian bookstores and distributors worldwide.

Cover design by: Prodigy Pixel

For more information on foreign distributors, call 717-532-3040. Or reach us on the Internet: www.destinyimage.com

Previous Published ISBN 0-7684-2224-8

ISBN 13: HC 978-0-7684-0529-3
ISBN 13 EBook: 978-0-7684-9978-0

For Worldwide Distribution, Printed in the U.S.A.
1 2 3 4 5 6 7 8 9 10 11 /17 16 15 14

Dedication

To
Patty Beckerdite
A dear and much-loved friend.

An angel from
the other realm came and
strengthened me.

—LUKE 22:43

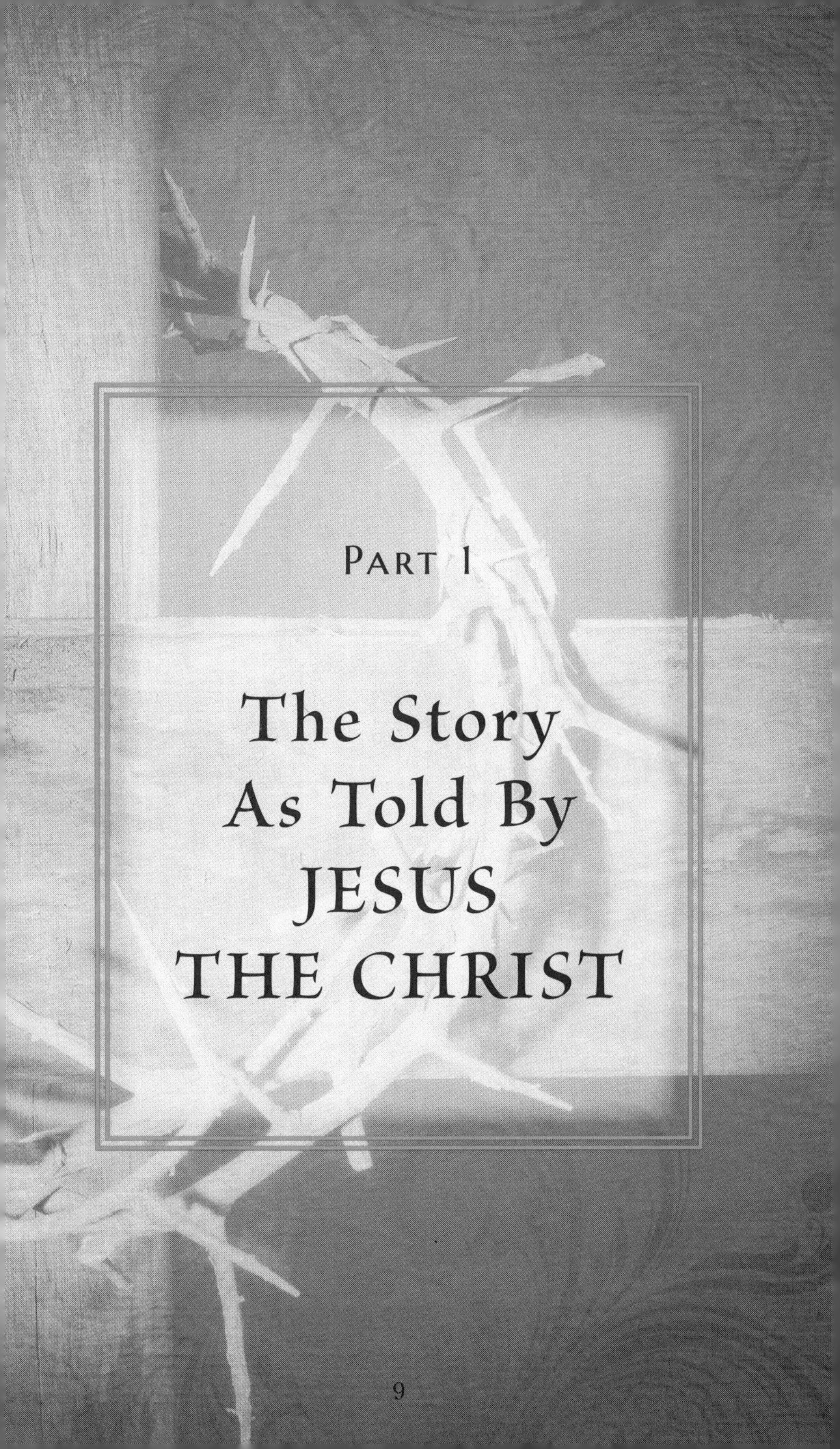

PART 1

The Story
As Told By
JESUS
THE CHRIST

Chapter 1

PILATE'S WIFE WAS having a fitful dream filled with disturbing images of angels and of innocent men going to their deaths.

Judas was making his way toward the Maccabaean Palace, trying hard not to think of what thirty pieces of silver might buy him.

The night was late, and my mother Mary felt her heart heavy and deeply troubled.

Over in a prison cell at Antonia's Fortress, three prisoners, each well chained, lay awake wondering what it would be like to have a nail driven through their hands and then to die of suffocation.

"The gnats and flies are the worst part, I was once told," came the voice of one of the thieves, breaking the silence of his dungeon.

"I do not need to know that," answered another.

Not far behind me, as I walked out of the city and crossed the Kidron Valley toward the Mount of Olives, Peter was finding it difficult to keep a small sword hidden under his robe.

A boy of seven, unable to find sleep, slipped out of his home and began wandering the city, hoping to find one of my disciples. He had a question to ask: "Why is this night so dark and foreboding?"

In the palace reserved for the governor of Galilee, Herod Antipas was not only awake, but drunk. I knew that before this night ended I would meet Herod face to face. I dreaded him, as snow dreads soot.

The Jewish leaders, who live mostly on the east side of the city, were in the process of making a decision concerning me which they knew had to be acted upon before the Passover Festival began. Once the sun rose, any decision might be too late.

The Gentiles, who live mostly on the west side of Jerusalem, would also face the same decision before noon of this same day.

As I reached my destination, an olive grove near the Mount of Olives, what concerned me most was that there was much activity stirring in the unseen realm among the principalities and powers.

Unaware of the treachery of this night, my disciples entered the olive grove with me, at a place where I often came to pray. Here in this grove I would know the last moments of freedom I would ever have while on this earth. I knelt and then fell to the ground. My disciples began to pray with me, but their prayers soon became labored. Shortly they fell asleep.

As I prayed, I wept. And as I wept, a cup appeared before me.

Though I had long known this hour would come, I recoiled in horror from what I beheld.

"Father! Please! If possible, find a way that I might not drink of it."

Even as I spoke, the cup drew nearer.

Chapter 2

THE CUP SPEWED its vile venom until the stench of its contents seemed to fill the winds of earth.

I watched as all the sins of all the sons of Abraham slipped into the cup. I saw their centuries of rebellion, idolatry, incest, murder, lies, and deceit make their way into the cup. The sins of the Hebrew race had now become one with that cup.

My hands and face began to pour forth blood until the ground around me was soaked.

I wept again. I called out for deliverance and cried, "Abba! Father!"

My body began to shake uncontrollably. So also my weeping and my cries of terror.

Never had I or any man known the depth of repulsion as I knew it when I saw the wantonness and evil that poured into that cup.

I would have surely died, but the door to the other realm opened, allowing an angel to come and minister to me. The image of the cup faded, but it would return. This time its images would be still more grotesque.

Struggling to my feet, I forced myself to return to my disciples. As I stood there, I marked the ground around me with my blood.

"You could not stay the night with me, could you?" I asked, as I returned to my place of prayer.

Father, permit even this.

Chapter 3

THIS TIME IT was not the transgressions of the sons of Abraham that I saw, but those of the heathen.

Within the cup's iniquitous brew I watched the sins of heathendom spill their idolatry, blasphemy, and the loathsomeness of all that the heathen imagination could conjure up. I cried, "Oh, the brutality of man toward man!" I saw the battles, the wars, the suffering, the pain—and the staggering depravity of heathendom. All found their way into the cup.

All the malfeasance of mankind, whether Jew or heathen, gathered into one place and disappeared within that cup.

All wickedness waited to mingle with all purity, all damnation calling out to envelop all righteousness, all that was heinous waiting to annihilate all holiness. All waited for me to yield to the cup.

Blood now flowed freely from my head, my face, my limbs. My very life force was racing to escape that which waited to become one with me. Mercifully, the cup once more withdrew.

Once more desirous to see my disciples, I struggled to stand, and then I collapsed. At last I came to them. Seeing them asleep, I could not but weep for each and all, even as I feared that every tear I shed would surely be my last.

Only by angels' graces was I able to return to my place of prayer and face that which lay ahead. As heinous as were the deeds of God's chosen people, as hideous as were the deeds of the heathen, all suddenly paled in the presence of the sin which I now beheld: the sin of the fallen creatures of the other realm. This moment was only the beginning of sorrow.

And so the cup returned.

Chapter 4

THE JEWS, YES. The heathen, yes. But, oh, must I drink the draught of the sin of the other realm?

No part of me could grasp the vastness of the incarnate evil which was forming before my eyes. It was not only my lot to behold the iniquities committed in the visible realm, but also those monstrous acts committed in realms unseen.

The cup trembled as the contents of the deeds of the fallen and accursed citizens of the unseen realm poured into the cup.

With unspeakable horror I watched the full corruption of the damned spirits, the foulness of the fallen angelic host, the perniciousness of the princes of perdition—all flowed into the vomitous brew.

"Oh, Father," I cried out with unutterable pain, "if there is any way, please remove this cup from me!"

Then in horrendous resignation I cried out, "But...if not...then...your...will...be...done."

Father, permit even this.

I collapsed to the ground which had become a pool of my own blood. An angel fought hard to stay my death, even the death of a broken heart and an emaciated body.

Chapter 5

THE CUP FADED once more, and for a moment I recalled an event which had taken place in past eternity, in a time before creation. I remembered a lamb—a lamb that was slain.

It was slain by my Father, in the age before the eternals. I was that lamb!

I was there in the Father, an offering made before creation. And now that slaying was about to join the physical creation, to join history, to join space and time.

For a moment my thoughts were suspended, both in eternity and in the olive grove. Gradually I found myself standing before eleven sleeping disciples. One of them cried out in a fitful dream and then fell back into a deep slumber.

Chapter 6

THE LONG BATTLE of surrender was over. My Father and I were in concert together.

I had been asked to drink the dregs of universal sin. I had yielded. Nonetheless, the horror of it was so great that it was beyond humankind to comprehend. In fact, not even Death himself could imagine what awaited me.

Once more I survived the ghastliness of it all only by the ministering of an angel.

Chapter 7

CAIAPHAS, THE HIGH priest, walked the long, narrow bridge that reached from the temple to the place of his residence. This bridge had been erected for the sole purpose of ensuring that a high priest would not touch anything unclean as he walked from the temple to his palace. Caiaphas was especially careful this particular night because it was so near to the hour of Passover.

In full priestly regalia, Caiaphas stepped off the bridge and onto The Pavement of Polished Stones. "Where is Judas? Is he on his way?" asked Caiaphas.

"He should arrive shortly," replied one of the temple guards.

"Have some of the Roman soldiers been enlisted to accompany the rest of the palace guard out to the grove?"

"They have."

"See to it that the Romans keep their distance from any of us.

"Are there swords? And torches? And, if necessary, clubs?"

"All three," came the reply.

"And you are certain all his disciples are with him?"

"At last sighting."

Caiaphas hesitated, then ordered, "Kill them if they resist.

"After the Galilean is brought here, there will be those who must witness against him. Have they all been properly prepared?"

"Yes, even as we speak."

"Then it is time to light the lamps and torches. Be on your way."

"When we arrive, how can we be certain which one is Jesus? It will be dark, and he wears no special clothing."

"Judas will kiss him."

With those words, Caiaphas started to return to his palace, but paused to ask: "One last question. Has the entire Sanhedrin been notified?"

"Yes, they are on their way. There are two whom we cannot locate."

"That is not a problem. Continue."

Just then Judas entered the courtyard.

Someone called out to him, "They are waiting for you. Join them immediately. It is yours to lead them to his place of prayer and to show them which one is Jesus."

Chapter 8

I SENSED THAT the son of perdition had now departed Jerusalem and was moving toward the Mount of Olives. Nor was he alone.

"Their hour has come," I whispered. "Father, I release my freedom, my will, my life, and soon my very spirit."

After all, this hour had long been established.

"Father, the cup: I will drink it."

The angel of mercy lifted me up in his arms once more until he was certain that I could walk. Just before departing, the angel wiped away the blood from my face.

"I must go from this place alone, angel of so great mercy; I must now dismiss you."

The angel nodded his head knowingly and obeyed, but not without protestation and tears: "When will it end, my Lord?"

"Not until Jonah is delivered," I replied.

"Quickly, retreat," I said to the angel for the last time.

I stood and began speaking to my Father.

Chapter 9

"Father, creation sprang forth from my hand

I fashioned the stars

I routed the heavens in their long run

Even as they vaulted across the chandeliers
of the sky

They reflected my glory

I scattered the iron in the strata of the earth

I brought forth the trees

That they might robe the earth in
emerald green

Upon that tree I now come

To end old Adam's race

And bring creation to its last page

death, confined by me within your cage

Soon to come forth in hell's own rage

One final sip of the frothing cup and receive
sin's final wage!

"Oh, Father, since my arrival upon this terrestrial ball I have dwelt in the confines of frail humanity. Extend to me sustaining grace even as death cries out to be released from his chains.

"Father, mingle my tears with your own."

I went to my slumbering disciples and said, "Arise. I must drink the cup."

Chapter 10

THEY STRUGGLED TO their feet and looked about. They saw no one they recognized.

"Where is Jesus? And who, pray tell, are you?"

Peter spoke again to the strange creature standing before him.

"Man, who or what can you be? Are you not blood? Or are you the dead come to visit us?"

At this point I replied, "Peter."

Peter thrust his hand across his mouth and cried, "My Lord! Oh, my Lord, is it really you? You are caked with blood! I recognize neither your face nor your frame."

James and John joined in a search to find words to express their consternation. How could a man have changed so much in so brief an hour? They did not know that in that ensuing hour I had won the everlasting title,

Man of Sorrows.

My sweat, my blood, and my garments had become one with my now-unrecognizable frame.

And so was fulfilled the prophecy I spoke to Isaiah long ago:

His appearance was beyond recognition as being a man. Isaiah 52:14

Ignoring their wonder, I motioned for my disciples to follow me. They hesitated, then followed.

John pressed toward my side. "I had a dream, I saw an angel. Did I see this? Was it a dream? Or did I truly see so strange a thing?"

"Come, John, you will know soon enough. There will come One to live within you who will remind you of this moment."

Noticing the faint light of distant torches, Peter began searching for his sword. He did not know the men bearing torches were seeking prey in the form of a criminal.

"Who would come to this place, and at such an hour?" asked James.

Just then John realized that someone was hiding in the shadows.

"John Mark, does your family know your whereabouts? What are you doing here?"

"I could not sleep," replied the lad. "On my way here, I saw guards everywhere. I think they are coming to get the Lord," continued the frightened youth.

"They have already arrived," I responded. "They have come to *my* Gethsemane. So also will each of you—for every man must one day face *his own* Gethsemane.

"My betrayer has arrived."

Chapter 11

"ROMAN SOLDIERS? GUARDS from the temple? Torches? Lanterns? A mob with clubs?" Thomas asked in wonderment. "And there are so many of them. It takes many a torch to light this strange darkness."

The crowd moved toward my disciples. With that, I stepped forward.

Judas, his black eyes darting everywhere, was trying to find his rabbi somewhere among the disciples. Suddenly his searching eyes stopped. For a long time he only stared. He studied my sandals and then my eyes. Cautiously, he edged toward me and raised a torch. "Is that you, Lord?"

Certain now that it was I, Judas leaned forward and kissed me on the cheek and then on my neck.

"It is by a kiss you betray me, Judas?"

Father, permit even this.

The soldiers were in confusion. They knew only that they were to watch for the one whom Judas kissed. "But surely," they thought, "there is some mistake." The mob had come expecting a prophet, someone tall, strong, and fearless. The vestige of this man they could not recognize.

"Whom do you seek?" I asked.

"We are looking for Jesus of Nazareth," said one of the soldiers, as he continued casting about from face to face.

"I am Jesus. I am the one you are seeking."

Until that moment the soldiers had not lingered upon the horror that was my face. Startled, they stumbled backward one upon another.

The captain of the temple guard, finally finding his discipline, ordered, "Bring rope."

Peter lunged.

Chapter 12

DRAWING A SWORD from beneath his garment, Peter swung wildly. He struck the ear of an unfortunate slave standing nearby. Quickly I replaced the ear. It had happened so suddenly that no one among the soldiers had time to react.

My angels had surrounded the olive grove and had drawn their swords. I whispered to the angelic host, "It is not for you to interfere. Return to the hilltops and prepare to return to the other realm on my command."

I then said to Peter, "If I needed help, I would have called forth my angels. This is not the time for battle, but for the cup."

I then searched the face of every person in the entire crowd. "Have you mistaken me for a thief? You have come out in such militant array? Surely you are seeking not me, but some desperate enemy of society. I have been with you openly in the temple, teaching *publicly* every day. Why did you not arrest me then?

"I will tell you why you have not arrested me until now. It is because it was not your hour. Now it is, but it is your only hour."

Glaring at me with triumphant hate, the mob then began to encircle me while eleven men disappeared into the night. The last to leave was the small boy named John Mark.

And now the freest creature ever to exist was bound and stripped of all rights and freedom.

I whispered to unseen ears, "Darkness, this is your hour. I am bound. I am in the hands of my chosen people. Soon I will be in the hands of the heathen. After that, I will find myself in your presence, oh you citizens of the inferno. The moment you have so long awaited is here."

But now I was in the most dangerous place imaginable: I was in the hands of *relig*ious men.

Chapter 13

A SOLDIER WALKED into the ironsmith's foundry.

"I have come for the nails."

"I have just finished them, and they are still warm. You will note that a few are more like spikes than nails, as you requested. Are they to be used in a crucifixion?"

"They are," observed the soldier. "I find them acceptable," he continued.

"Of course they are acceptable! The nails I forge here have been used in hundreds of crucifixions, crucifixions which stretch from the sea to the desert."

"But I have a question for you," inquired the soldier: "That first set of nails was ordered by the Romans, but the last ones were ordered by the Sanhedrin. Why the Sanhedrin? It is unlawful. The Sanhedrin will not dare kill anyone, especially by crucifixion. Only Romans can do that. The Sanhedrin cannot order an execution, much less a crucifixion."

"Oh, yes, they can. At least when they are this sure of themselves," the ironsmith answered. "Today they are a determined lot."

"I also need four crossbeams."

"Four?"

"Yes. Three for some robbers and one for a man called Jesus. He is some local prophet of sorts."

"Jesus?"

"The same."

"You know, do you not, that he claims to be the Son of God."

"God? Which one? We Romans have many!"

"We have only one."

"One?"

"But how could he allow himself to be crucified by his own creative handiwork if he is the Son of God, the one who created this iron and fashioned the trees? That is what troubles me about that strange man."

"Well, it does not trouble the Sanhedrin," retorted the soldier as he turned to leave.

"Will you Romans also be needing stakes for the crossbeams?"

"No. We plan to use a tree this time. One on the Mount of Olives."

The ironsmith then loaded four crossbeams onto a cart.

"Cursed is the man who hangs on a tree," muttered the troubled ironsmith. "Is it possible that the Son of God would be on such a tree?"

Chapter 14

THE GUARDS LED me out of the olive grove, on to the home of Annas, the oldest of the high priests.

The sons of Abraham were about to place me on trial.

"The prisoner has arrived," reported someone to Annas.

As I waited, I heard a servant say, "Is that grotesque figure over there Jesus? If it is, why bother with a trial, he is already virtually dead."

Annas smoothed his robes and came toward me. He studied my face carefully and then thought to himself, "It will be a short walk from here to this man's death.

"Son of Joseph and Mary, why do you proclaim treachery and sedition to the people? What have you been teaching your followers?" demanded Annas.

I responded, "You do not need to ask me that question. You only need to ask those who have heard me speak."

At that instant I received a hard blow to the mouth from a temple guard. "You are speaking to the high priest, criminal!" What the guard did not know was that he had just struck the true high priest.

The words of Caiaphas in an earlier comment rang in Annas's ear:

"This man's followers grow by the day. There will be a day when he will try to set up his kingdom in Israel. When that happens, Rome will remove our status as a peaceful nation. Rome will dissolve the Sanhedrin, seize our many holdings, and the Roman sword will slaughter thousands of people. It is far better for one to die for all."

With that, Annas sent me to the home of Caiaphas, where the Sanhedrin began to gather, along with a number of Pharisees and Sadducees.

"Come to the center of the courtyard, you whom all Israel fears," called one of the priests. "He is not much to look at, is he? Did people actually listen to this man?

"Have the Romans beaten him already? They were not supposed to, not until we were through with him!"

"No, they have not; nor have the Jews," replied one of the temple guards.

"Then what happened to this poor soul?"

"I do not know. I have seen this man before, but tonight I would not have recognized him."

Caiaphas asked a similar question. "Are you sure it is Jesus?"

Being assured that it was Jesus, he whispered to one of the guards, "Have them bring in the witnesses."

For a long while Caiaphas questioned me. I saw in his eyes that he was troubled concerning the success or failure of this night's attempt to kill me.

I said nothing.

The witnesses were brought in. After much contradicting testimony, Annas slipped over to Caiaphas and whispered, "We will never convince Pilate that this man ought to be put to death with what little we have here. What can I do with witnesses who cannot keep their stories straight?"

"There is one thing you can do," whispered a priest in his ear.

"Tell me," responded Caiaphas.

"Adjure him."

"But what if he lies?" retorted Caiaphas.

"This man does not lie." The words struck Caiaphas like an arrow.

At that, Caiaphas took a deep breath, and speaking loudly for all to hear, he pronounced: "I adjure you by the living God, are you the Messiah? Are you the Son of God?"

Before answering, I looked around the courtyard and stared into the faces of every priest, rabbi, scribe, Pharisee, and Sadducee present. I looked at Caiaphas and then at the temple guards. All were nervous. I then raised my eyes toward the nearby hills where stood ten thousand heavenly angels, each with his hand upon his sword, awaiting a word from me. That word never came.

"He has been adjured," whispered one of the angels.

"Will he finally reveal who he is?" asked another.

Finally my eyes again met those of the high priest. With a calm that had been mine throughout all eternity, I spoke those forbidden words:

I AM.

"Furthermore," I continued, "a day is coming when you will see the Son of *Man* return here with his angels, descending in a cloud of glory."

An angel whispered, "Lord, hasten that day."

As soon as Caiaphas heard my words, he grabbed his garment and began tearing it. In feigned rage he began screaming. "Blasphemy! Who needs more evidence? This Galilean has witnessed against himself! He has blasphemed against our God. It is with his own tongue he has pronounced his own death sentence. This heretic is exactly what we believed him to be, a man not worthy of life."

Caiaphas turned and addressed the Sanhedrin. "I call for a verdict. For myself, I am certain this Nazarene is not worthy to live out this day. God is with us. I mean to see this man dead before Passover begins," he vowed.

Silently I spoke to the angels, "Return to your realm." I would not see them again until I heard the grinding of a huge stone being rolled away.

The ordeal had taken the entire night.

It was 5:00 a.m.

Chapter 15

WHILE THE VERDICT was being pronounced, there was something else taking place near the Judean hills. A solitary priest was making his way up the steps to one of the pinnacles of the temple. Once there, he turned east and searched the horizon. Below him lay the temple courtyard, choked with expectant pilgrims, while late arrivers were pushing their way through the twenty-four entrances of the temple grounds.

The priest continued studying the landscape, straining to see past the slopes of the Mount of Olives, across the open fields, on to Bethany, and beyond.

The priest watched as yet other sojourners who had come by sea were now pressing their way into Jerusalem through the western gates. He turned again toward the east. For a moment he stood motionless. At that moment the tip of the sun broke over the horizon, lighting the eastern hills. With that, the priest cried out, "The morning sun!"

From below, another priest called up to him, "How far can the morning light be seen? As far as Hebron?" came his traditional inquiry.

"Yes," came the reply, "even as far as Hebron."

The crowd below began to applaud. Scores of priests, in unison, raised silver trumpets and filled the air with a loud blast of the sacred horns. The pilgrims standing below cheered.

The regular morning sacrifice, observed every day of the year, began. A tiny lamb was led to a golden bowl of water, that it might take a last drink, and was then led to the altar of sacrifice.

Just as the lamb was being tied to the altar, so my hands were being tied.

I hardly listened as the Sanhedrin's verdict was announced. "By Hebrew law this heretic is to die." They could not possibly realize that this verdict had been established long ago in the eternal past.

With the rising of the sun and completion of the morning sacrifice, the Passover Festival began. It would end at 6:00 p.m.

In twelve hours the Passover lamb would be slain. Both men and principalities knew I *must* be dead before that hour.

I had nine hours to live. These would be the most awful hours ever lived by man.

It was now 6:00 a.m.

Chapter 16

"Gillepha!"

"Blasphemer," they called me.

The Sanhedrin, as one, began to pelt me with questions. I answered not a word.

Finally, the inquisition ended. I was then turned over to the temple guard.

Murder by slow torture had begun.

"Your soldiers must understand that this man must be dead before nightfall," ordered Caiaphas. "Beat this man, and beat him well. Nor do I want any pity shown. Make sure that he is even more grotesque looking than now. When you are finished with the whip, take him to Pilate."

"I thought he had already been beaten," murmured another of the guards.

Suddenly I was hit with a terrible blow that knocked me across the room. Then another and then another.

I yielded to all that followed. A crucifixion *is*, after all, a crucifixion.

The temple guards, as one, then began to spit on me.

Another blow, then another. The corridor was filled with mock laughter followed by mock sympathy. When that ceased to amuse them, they blindfolded me. Again I was hit hard with a fist, then another.

"Prophesy, Son of God. Tell us the name of the one who hit you. Now tell us who is *about* to hit you."

Obscene words filled the room.

The rope tied around my hands was fastened to a ring set in the wall.

My clothes were removed.

The beating began.

Lash followed lash as my back and legs turned red. Then my skin began to tear open. Soon, from my neck to my legs I was a ribbon of ripped flesh.

When they finally cut me down, the beating and the spittle continued.

Just as Caiaphas ordered, my open wounds, which reached as deep as my bones, flowed with blood. My swollen face was sliced and tattered. I appeared to be far less than a human being.

While lying on the floor, I could hear the Sanhedrin plotting their next move. "We must take this blasphemer to Pilate in such a way that he must order immediate execution," they concluded.

I was hauled before them and questioned again. They were hoping to find a greater charge against me. Not one among them cared for my tortured condition. The only answer I gave them was similar to the last. "You will see me sitting at God's right hand. From there I will return in the clouds."

The entire Sanhedrin decided that there was strength in numbers and that they would march together over to Pilate's residence. I was forced to follow in fetters.

I had been judged by the Jews. I was about to be judged by the heathens.

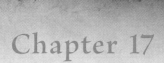

Chapter 17

AS THE SANHEDRIN stepped into the Jerusalem streets, they met with a wall of celebrating humanity that blocked their passage. The guards pushed hard against the throng until finally they edged their way to Antonia's Fortress.

"My lamb. See my lamb," called out a child. "The priest could find no flaw in him."

Everywhere I looked, people were carrying a snow-white lamb. The stream of whiteness flowed steadily toward the temple. All that surrounded me seemed to take on a white purity.

I also heard the bleating of lambs being led to slaughter.

When a child caught a glimpse of my face, he cried out, and ran in terror.

Father, permit even this.

Suddenly, I heard a voice coming from a place not of this earth.

"My Son, you have been judged by my chosen people. You were rejected—rejected by the Hebrews first. Always they are first. In a few moments you will be judged by all that there is of mankind that is not Hebrew. In so doing, you will fill up all the condemnation of Adam's race. *After that* will come those creatures who live in places unseen. Then shall all judgment be complete, and salvation shall be to the uttermost."

The voice faded as we arrived at Pilate's palace. The Sanhedrin filed into Pilate's outdoor courtyard in order not to make themselves unclean.

I thought: "Arrest me without cause, try me illegally, rehearse false witnesses, then plot to murder me, yet all this does not make the Sanhedrin unclean? So it is with religious men."

"Why do you bring this man to me? Take him and judge him according to Hebrew law."

"We want him dead, and you know that only a Roman can order a man's death."

"What is his crime?" asked Pilate impatiently.

"He is claiming to be a king. He is also inciting the people, telling them not to pay their taxes."

Pilate, a superstitious man, only heard one word, *king*. He then ordered me inside his palace.

"Are you some kind of king?"

"I am. However, my kingdom cannot be seen; it is above, in a place where all things are invisible. Nonetheless, a king I am, and I came to this planet for that very purpose."

Strange, is it not, that on this day, the only person who would attempt to save me from death was a heathen governor.

Chapter 18

IN THE HOURS that followed, five times Pilate sought to save me from the Sanhedrin. Hearing their charges that I had stirred up people in Galilee, Pilate saw an opportunity. He blinked. "Galilee?! This man is a Galilean?" Pilate turned to one of his assistants, "Is not Herod in Jerusalem at his residence?"

"He is."

"Ah, ha! That old reprobate. If I know him, he is drunk—and more! Quickly, send this man to Herod Antipas. Have him speak to this Galilean. As surely as I live, Herod knows of this man. Who knows! Perhaps he even knows the truth!"

To the utter dismay of the Sanhedrin, I was quickly ushered over to Herod, governor of Galilee.

It was difficult for me to stand before that man. His father, Herod the Great, had sent thousands of babies to their deaths during the time of my birth. And Herod himself had ordered the beheading of my cousin John.

"I hear you are quite a magician; I hear you even perform miracles. Here! Give me a sign!"

I looked away.

"I can have you set free," slurred Herod.

Once more I looked away.

Herod was dismayed. He had looked forward to meeting me. "I will waste no more time with this one, even if he claims to be a king."

Hearing that I claimed to be a king, a soldier placed a purple robe across my shoulders. They jeered and mocked, calling me "King! King of the Jews!" When this was no longer humorous, I was escorted back to Pilate.

Just as we moved into the street, I heard Herod call out, "Tell Pilate this man has done no wrong."

Seeing me again, Pilate announced, "Herod concurred with me that this man is innocent!"

Searching again for a way out, yet underestimating the religious leaders' determination to kill me, Pilate declared, "I will give this man a good beating; then I will set him free."

This only made the leaders more incensed. Their charges against me escalated.

In the midst of all the accusations against me, my silence stunned Pilate.

The crowd pushed its way as close to Pilate as they could. At that moment a guard handed a message from Pilate's wife.

"Have nothing to do with this innocent man. I had a terrible nightmare concerning him."

More determined than ever to set me free, Pilate tried another possibility. "I am about to set one man free: a murderer and insurrectionist against Rome, or your king. Which is your pleasure?"

Pilate was nothing less than amazed at the response of the deeply religious and moral men: "Give us Barabbas!" they responded as one.

Pilate breathed hard and thought to himself: "Surely if I bring out both men, and the people see the hardened criminal and the beaten, swollen, half-dead body of the peasant, the Sanhedrin will relent."

I was keenly aware that I was now on trial before the visible principalities. The chosen people must condemn me, and then the heathen would. And after that I must also stand before yet another tribunal and be rejected.

Barabbas raised a clenched fist. Pilate grabbed his arm and called out, "Will you have me release Barabbas, or Jesus who is called the Messiah?"

One of the priests chanted, "Barabbas! Release Barabbas!"

Pilate shouted angrily, "Envy! All that is here is envy! I just told you that this man is not guilty."

The leaders responded in kind. "This man must die. Anyone claiming to be the Son of God must die!"

Aware that he was dealing with no ordinary man, when Pilate heard the word *God*, he panicked. Ordering me back into his residence, Pilate, with ashen face and trembling voice, demanded, "Who are you?!"

I said nothing.

My silence once more mystified Pilate.

"Do you not know that I have the authority to set you free or to crucify you? Say something!"

I replied, "You are a government official, an envoy of Rome; nonetheless, you have no authority. You have authority only because it is given you from my heavenly Father."

Pilate again tried to release me.

"If you release Jesus, you are no friend of Caesar. This man claims to be a king and therefore is a rebel against Caesar," charged the Jewish leaders.

Pilate returned to the judgment seat, and once more I stood before the mob. Pilate declared, "Here is the man! I bring him to you, but know that I do not find him guilty!"

The leading priests were the first to shout, "Crucify him!"

Pilate retorted, "What? Crucify your king?"

With lies and flattery on their tongues, men who utterly despised the Roman conquest were crying, "We have no king but Caesar!"

"I cannot believe this! This is turning into a riot."

According to Roman law, if a riot breaks out on peaceful soil, the governor is sent back to Rome in shame. Resigned to the injustice of the hour, Pilate called for a basin of water. "Hear my words, Sanhedrin, I am innocent of this man's blood. You crucify him!"

The crowd cheered, "Then let his blood be on our heads!"

The soldiers led me to a small room in the fortress called the Praetorium. The entire battalion had come to watch.

Earlier, when I stood before Herod, his guards had placed a purple robe about me. Now when the Roman guards (whose charge was to flog me) saw the robe of royal purple, they also mocked me with it.

Once again I was stripped naked. One soldier took several branches of thorns and wove them into a single thorn-encrusted wreath. While others cheered, the soldier rammed the crown of thorns onto my head, tearing into my scalp and forehead as he did. Once more my blood was splattered everywhere.

Next they gave me a wooden stick, declaring, "Behold your scepter. Rule, King! Rule! I kneel before you, King of the Jews."

Then they grabbed the stick and beat me with it.

I had now been beaten by the heathens as well as the chosen. At last the flogging ended. My body was not so much wounded as it was itself a wound.

They took me to the cells where the other condemned were awaiting their executions.

Barabbas, who was being led out of the prison, passed my cell on his way to freedom. He stopped and looked in. Seeing my condition he called out, "God, what have you done to that man?"

"What we did?" replied a soldier, "We almost beat him to death. But he looked almost this bad when the Jews gave him to us. Nonetheless, be assured, Barabbas, we will see you back here in less than a week. We are laying bets we will get a second chance to crucify you."

As they pushed Barabbas further down the hall, there was a brief moment when I was alone. I was shivering violently.

Chapter 19

"WHERE WILL IT be?" asked one of the guards as they passed my cell.

"On one of the hills overlooking Jerusalem. The one facing the temple. The high priest insisted on that particular place. He said this man's last sight would be that of the entrance to the temple."

"I am not surprised. It has to do with a proverb."

"A proverb?"

"Yes, a Jewish proverb. When a man claims to be the Messiah, they say to him, 'Prove it by ripping down the temple veil.' "

"If he can do that while hanging on a cross, I would be inclined to believe him myself," replied the soldier.

"Are they to be hung on stakes or on trees?"

"There is a particular old tree up there on the crest of the Mount of Olives. It is dead, bleached white, and hard as stone. We can hang all three of them on the same tree."

"What about the patibula? Where are they?"

"A local smith has made the nails and the crossbeams."

The captain of the guard walked into my cell. "I doubt we will need three crossbeams today. That carpenter may not live long enough for us to hang him."

Then the captain of the guard called out to some of the other soldiers, "What is that?"

"It is his robe. We took it off when he first arrived here."

The captain stared at it. "*His* robe? I have never seen anything like it. A robe with no seams."

"It was given to me by my mother," I replied.

"He can speak," said the captain, hesitating to even look in the direction of my voice.

"After he is dead you can gamble for it, but only after he is dead, not before. And let there be no fighting over his robe. Your charge is to crucify him, not to fight over his clothes. As I said, gamble for it."

Lying there on the cold floor once more, I heard my Father speaking to me.

"Golgotha will become not only the place of *your* execution, my son, but the execution of the sin of this world. Furthermore, the cross of Golgotha will be the instrument for destroying all creation."

Chapter 20

"Is he dead?" asked the soldier as he swung open the door.

"Worse than dead, but bring him out. The others will be right behind us."

I staggered to my feet and then leaned hard against the wall. I was not at all sure that I would live long enough to be crucified.

A squad of four soldiers entered the dank room.

"Take the crossbeam and place it on his shoulders."

"Galilean, you carry *your own* instrument of death. Such are the ways of us Romans when we crucify men. It is to be a lesson for all onlookers."

"Do you understand that you are being taken to the cross?" asked a soldier, not sure I could even hear him.

"Yes," I replied. "I have understood the ways of the Cross for a very long time."

"Can he carry it?"

"Does it matter? This whip will see that he does!"

"Can a whip make a dead man walk?" the other soldier retorted.

They led me down the hall and into the daylight. The brightness of the sun was excruciating. "This was not an hour for light," I heard myself say.

I knelt as they placed the splintered wood across my shoulder. I struggled hard to remain balanced. I did not have the strength to stand. Then came the whip. Then again. And again. Finally, by graces lent me from another world, I stood. In the brightness of the morning I could see the path which would lead me to a hill and on it a place called The Skull.

I clutched the wooden beam in my bloodied hands.

The guards led me around the city walls until we came to the western gate, where they pointed me toward the Mount of Olives.

"The crowd is so thick," complained one of the guards, "but it will open when they hear my whip."

With that, I heard the crack of a Roman whip splitting the air. The crowd fell back.

For but a moment I could see as far as Bethany. Every family was carrying an unblemished, snowy white lamb.

A moment later, I passed a group of women waiting for me beside the road. They were weeping uncontrollably.

"It is not for me you should weep," I said. "They have done this when the tree was green; consider what they will do when it is dry."

"Push them aside," ordered one of the soldiers.

"He will never make it up that hill," grumbled one of the guards, "especially against this crowd."

I collapsed again.

"Find one or two people to help this Jew, otherwise it will take hours to get to the top of that hill."

"You two, there, come here," the solider yelled.

One of the men looked up in terror.

"Pick up that crossbeam and take hold of that man there. Drag him up that hill," the soldier ordered.

The man protested, "I will not touch that, even if you beat me!"

"But you are not even a Jew. I told you to pick him up."

"Jew or Gentile, I have standards. I will not touch… that…whatever it is."

"Ha! Jews are not supposed to touch a Gentile. Here is a Gentile who will not touch a Jew!"

"You! The other one. Pick up this man."

The soldier raised his whip.

"A whip is not needed," came a soft, strong voice. "I will help him."

"It does not serve you well to stand out in a crowd, does it?" chided the soldier. "Where are you from?"

"I am from Cyrene."

He then reached down to help me to my feet. "I will carry his cross," he added.

"No, you will not! That is forbidden. He will have to die in order to escape carrying his cross. But you are allowed to help him."

"What is your name?" I asked.

"I am Simon called Niger. I am of Cyrene."

With that, Simon reached down and grasped the beam of wood. The soldier forced me to my feet.

"Niger? Simon of Cyrene?" I said, as we struggled forward together.

"Sir, you do not know me?!"

"Simon of Cyrene?" I asked again.

"You do know me?"

"Yes, I have always known you."

"But I do not know you," he blinked.

"Do you not have two sons?"

"Yes," replied the astonished man.

"Are they not called Alexander and Rufus?" I inquired.

"You *do* know me," replied Simon in disbelief. "When have we met? I have no memory of you. How long did you say you have known me? How long have I known you?"

"We met long, long ago, before the foundation of the world.

"A few weeks from now you will begin to follow me. A few years later, you will flee this city under persecution. You will travel westward until you come to the sea. You, your wife and your two children will then proclaim me to the heathen."

"Sir, you are mad."

"Perhaps," I replied. "Let us wait and see. A day is coming when you will remember my words."

Simon looked into my deeply-scarred face, and there, in spite of his disbelief, he believed.

Again, I spoke to him, "Simon, from this day forward I will ever be a guest—not in your home, but within your heart."

Not understanding what was just said, yet somehow knowing, Simon deliberately lifted the crossbeam and moved forward.

The guard stared.

Calmly Simon spoke to the guard, "If you raise that whip again, let its lashes fall upon me."

The soldier, unaccustomed to such frontal defiance, let the whip fall to his side.

Twelve soldiers, three men judged worthy of death, and a conscripted African slowly made their way toward the crest of a hill.

At last I came to Golgotha.

I turned to face the temple. I also saw the temple courtyard filled with families holding their lambs awaiting sacrifice.

Like most people, Simon had previously witnessed the Roman way of dealing with executions. Upon arriving at the top of the hill, Simon dropped the crossbeam on the ground and then laid me next to it. We both knew what would soon follow.

As Son of Man, it now fell to me to hasten the drama. I spoke to the skies and beyond:

"It is your hour, powers of darkness. Prepare to come here at my command. The Jews have tried me. The heathen have tried me. Now it is your turn."

It was almost noon.

Chapter 21

"HERE ARE TWO of the criminals. It is time to begin."

"You two, each of you stand beside your crossbeam. Now lie down on it and stretch out your arms."

"What about that third one over there?"

"Do not bother with him. He will be dead before the nails get to him."

With that, the twelve soldiers drew their swords and formed a semi-circle around their three prisoners. This was a signal to all bystanders that under no circumstances were they to interfere with these executions. Anyone who dared would be instantly cut down.

I stared again at the piece of wood. "My Cross," I said faintly, "you are but a piece of wood, but you are about to destroy creation itself."

Again, I spoke to the unseen realm, "Meet me here, principalities and powers. Come. It is your destiny to meet me at my Cross."

Then I spoke to the city below. "Jerusalem, you have so often slain your prophets."

Next I beheld the temple. I saw the covered entrance which had blocked the view of its sacred chambers. And beyond that, the veil. Beyond the veil, the Holy of Holies. The last sight I would behold would not be the Holy of Holies, but the Ark itself!

After my death I would yet lay my eyes on another door, the one that separates heaven from earth. After this day, the separation would be no more.

I then searched the surrounding hills, for there was yet another scene. At last I sighted the *scapegoat*, all alone on the side of a hill, fastened to a small altar.

"Hear me scapegoat," I said. "This day you and I have been led outside the camp. You the picture, and I the one who is truly *the scapegoat*. You are tied to an altar and cannot move. So I, too, am about to be tied to my altar."

Having said that, I lay down on the crossbeam and stretched out my arms.

Father, permit even this.

The soldiers stared at me. In all their experiences of executing men, they had never seen the victim willingly stretch out his arms to receive the nails.

It was I and I alone who would consent to the Cross. I opened my palms.

The soldier paused, still expecting me to resist. But my arms and hands simply waited.

"So should all men receive the Cross," I whispered.

"Mad, that is what you are," grunted the soldier.

"Mad?" asked Simon. "Has any man faced with crucifixion met that fate with such dignity?"

The sky began to darken.

Simon searched the skies. "Those are the blackest clouds I have ever seen. They seem to be billowing out from some other world. I feel some dreadful unnatural thing is happening." He shuddered, "It is as if all the wickedness of time and eternity were moving toward this hill.

"What is his crime?" Simon asked.

"As far as I can tell," answered one of the soldiers, "the greatest crime this man ever committed was to hew a chair and make a table."

"I do not understand."

"The man I am about to nail to that piece of wood is a peasant from the countryside, from Galilee. He is a carpenter."

"Of the gods," murmured one of the newly-arrived guards as he put his hand onto his mouth, "is that the man we are killing this day? I have heard him. I have seen him. Do you realize that we may put to death a king, a real king?"

"Never mind, kings die the same way thieves do. This is your first time to crucify someone, is it not, soldier?"

"It is, but I have a notion it will not be the last."

"Look over there at the Jews' temple. See all those people? We are looking at them, but they are also looking at us! At six this evening they will slaughter vast numbers of lambs. Frankly, until then we will be the main event of the day. You will have a good view of their Passover festivities, and they have a good view of our slaughter of a man."

"Watching this man die a hideous death may be more interesting to them than slaying a lamb."

At that moment came a loud yell. One of the thieves, trying to delay the nails, called out, "Who is this man over here? He does not look like Barabbas to me! He does not look like anything. Where is Barabbas? He should be dying beside me. And that thing lying next to me, is that a human being?"

"Barabbas is free."

Swear words split the wind. "He got away again?"

"Yes, thanks to this one who will die with you, Barabbas got away. Pilate set Barabbas free. More to the truth, this man set Barabbas free."

"Who is this man that he can set another man free?"

"Whoever he is he *cannot* set *you* free," taunted the soldier.

"What is his name?"

The other thief joined in. "Yes, who is he? I am particular with whom I die."

The Roman guards laughed at the thief's macabre humor. "Whoever he is, and whatever they have done to him, his own mother would not recognize him now."

"Not true," came the gentle voice of an elderly lady standing nearby. "I do recognize him, and I know exactly who he is," she added.

"What did he do, murder someone?" the thief continued.

Another soldier replied, "This criminal committed a worse crime than all of you. You only robbed and murdered. This one claims to be the Son of God. Worse still, he challenged the institutions. No man should ever be so great a fool."

The thief asked again defiantly, "Who is this man?"

"It does not matter. You only need to know he will die the same way you will. If he is a king, he will die, if he is a dog he will die, if he is a Jew he will die, if he is a Gentile like you he will die. If he is God Himself, he will still die. Now, both of you either lie down or be knocked down."

Just then a mounted soldier arrived on the scene. Seeing one last chance to forego the nails, the thief asked the horseman, "What crime did this man commit?"

"Last week he was a hero. Tens of thousands came out to greet him on the Bethany road. They threw palm branches before him. That was last week. This week he is the enemy of Israel and Rome."

One of the thieves looked at me and exclaimed, "Man, what did you do this week?"

"He claimed to be the Messiah. The problem was, for many he proved he really was! Now, mind my words or know the whip."

The two thieves began to struggle. Both were pushed to the ground, their arms forced down and tied to the beams of wood.

In the meantime, I continued to wait. I was lying on a cross which my Father had endowed with the power to annihilate the universe.

One of the soldiers came to my side and began to probe my wrist and hand.

"Simon?" I called quietly.

Niger slipped beside me.

"I am about to be crucified, but something else will happen which you will not see. In a little while you will depart this hill and return to your family, but in the eyes of my Father you will be one with me on this cross. In my Father's reckoning (and that is the only reckoning that matters) you will be crucified with me."

"But you said in a few days I would be one of your followers. I cannot do that and also die today."

"In God's eyes this will happen. You will be crucified with me, but you will go on living. From now on you will not live by human life; you will live by divine life. My Father's life will live your life."

That ended the conversation. The crucifixion proceedings had begun.

Then came that grizzly cry of men having nails being hammered through their hands and fettered to wood. The two men were still screaming hideously when soldiers steadied their ladders and pulled the two men up to the tree. One was nailed facing north; the other was facing south.

Oaths and blasphemies continued. The weight of both men was suspended on no more than those nails. If it was possible to be more horrible, even more horrible wails were heard as each man then had a single nail pierce both feet. Each man then had his feet and legs tied firmly to the tree.

Deep within me I silently cried out, "Oh, My Father, what is about to happen, do not let it be hindered by my will."

As one soldier pressed my wrist, another steadied the nail. Then came the dull thud of a hammer smashing the nail as it ripped through my wrist. Blood spurted upon the swearing soldiers, across my arms and upon my face.

As silently as a lamb being led to slaughter, I uttered not a word.

"He is not resisting. This is a sight I have never seen."

Once more I felt the soldier probing my other wrist.

Then again came the sound of tearing flesh and sinews. Once more my blood spewed all over the Roman guards.

The wails of the two now-crucified thieves continued to fill the air, as did their curses against man and God.

"Shut up, thief!" called out one of the soldiers. "Be content that you are about to die with God."

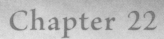

Chapter 22

BOTH MY HANDS were now fastened firmly to the cross-beam. Now it was time to hoist me up to the tree.

"Steady the ladders," someone said.

They began pulling the crossbeam upward. For a long unbearable moment I was suspended in air. Finally the cross was tied to the tree.

"Hang me on the west side of the tree," I requested.

"What did he say?"

"He wants to face the temple."

"That is a small request for a dead man. Hang him on the west side."

Like the chosen sheep now being led into the temple for slaughter, I uttered not a word.

To be certain the nails in my wrist would hold, they took rope and tied my arms, and then they tied the cross-beam to the tree. I felt two soldiers grab my feet, pressing both legs together, heel on top of heel.

"Hand me that longest nail and the hammer."

I felt the spike being pressed against my ankles.

"You will scream this time, prophet," growled one of the soldiers.

The nail was slammed repeatedly as it gradually ripped my flesh, through one heel, then the other, on its way to the tree.

I moaned quietly.

"A king so meek," said one of the soldiers. "No wonder they feared him so."

My legs were then tied to the tree.

I was now the brazen serpent lifted up to cure all mankind.

The soldiers were about to climb down from their ladders when the mounted guard ordered them to wait. "We are not finished here. Take this piece of wood with a sign written by Pilate himself. Nail the sign above the Jew. Make sure that all can see it clearly."

One of the soldiers stared at the wooden board.

"It is in three languages."

"Yes, three."

The soldier then nailed the wooden sign to the tree. "Such an unmentionable crime," he said facetiously.

Everyone nearby began reading the sign.

Jesus of Nazareth—King of the Jews

Satisfied, the soldier spoke again: "Earlier, out near Pilate's courtyard, the Jewish leaders protested the words he had written. They wanted it to read, 'He claimed to be king of the Jews.' Pilate would have none of it. He replied emphatically, 'I wrote what I wrote.'"

"What does the sign say?" cried out one of the thieves. "What does it say?" he demanded to know.

"It says you are dying beside an Israelite king."

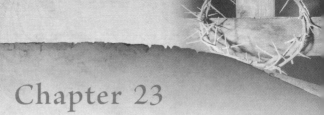

Chapter 23

THE SUN WAS now high above the eastern hills. On the walls surrounding the temple a priest cried out to the pilgrims, "From whence have you come?"

"They come from the ends of the earth," was the traditional reply.

Just after that, Caiaphas made his way out of his residence and stared toward the Mount of Olives to be certain all was going according to his plan.

"The last thing you will see will be the entrance to the temple, perhaps even the curtained door," he said quietly, speaking to himself. "Let us see if you can rip down the sacred curtain. Let us see you open the way to the Holy of Holies."

Chapter 24

ONLY EYES WHICH can see that which cannot be seen could know the drama that next began unfolding on the hill. Time ceased its onward march. Mass, space, and time came to a halt. I was now looking into the gathering of creatures that man's eyes cannot see.

The cloud over Golgotha grew thicker and more foreboding.

Everywhere, pictures, types, and symbols surrounded me. The Passover, the temple, the lamb—all had been but shadows of me. The gathering darkness made clear that the shadows, types, and symbols were about to find their fulfillment.

The pernicious citizens of perdition had arrived. I heard a voice. I knew it well.

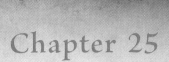

Chapter 25

OUT OF THE abyss of darkness I heard a voice as beautiful as the voice of an angel. "Fallen monsters of the unseen worlds, come to me," I commanded. The first of three whom I called came toward me.

"Carpenter," flowed the smooth words.

"I know you. Your slaves are innumerable," I answered.

"Yes," replied the entrancing voice of the World System. "Should you be surprised? I am the power of all systems."

"You are the World System itself," I chided. "You are chief enslaver of all mankind."

"Carpenter, you know me well. I came into being soon after the fall of Adam. His descendents had no choice but to come to me, having lost the favored state of your fellowship. And do not forget, you are the one who forced Adam out of the Garden. Something had to fill the void. I found it my duty to help those forsaken souls. It is only by their choice that I enslave every son of Adam who was ever born.

"Ah, but best of all, they know not their chains. They cry freedom even as they drag their fetters through life."

"Why are you here, worldliness?" I asked.

"Ah, I have come to watch you die. And as you die, I want you to know that the entire system of the world will henceforth hold within its clutches the enslavement of all mankind—forever!"

"Your beauty is for the moment. Furthermore, it is only for the blind."

"Ah, but my trinkets and tinsel are so alluring! Men cannot wait to possess them.

"Know this well, Carpenter: After you are dead, *your kingdom is v*anquished.

"All spend a lifetime trying to find happiness and approval, and oh, how they envy the false god of success. All the while they pursue success, they weave their own chains. Fools and slaves, ever pursuing the elusive narcotic of success.

"See them! My vast galley of slaves! They work a lifetime for me, yet their riches are but rags. Systems within systems, ever binding but always disappointing. Beautiful, all are so beautiful, the compelling promises, dreams, and hopes. False promises, I am. But they rush to me eagerly, generation after endless generation."

Worldliness laughed with the satisfaction only a slave master knows when he ensnarls his prey. "They complain when my promises are found empty, but they never blame me. Ha! And they complain as bitterly when riches do come. Wealth, power, fame, and adoration they crave, but slavery is the husk I serve at every party.

"Withered wreaths. Elusive happiness. Do you not know, Carpenter, that this race you created will, for a moment of adulation, gladly sell their souls?!

"But the conquest I desire the most is the one I come for at this hour. Upon your death shall die the threat of any competition. Die, Carpenter, and in a moment my system shall pervade all creation. I shall be enslaver of all. True freedom will vanish from the memory of mankind. All men will be in the web of my world systems. I will be the one and only 'way of life'! Earth will be but a prison, and civilization will be my keep.

"Poor Son of God, you came here thirty years ago to this earth, thinking that there would grow up among the redeemed a people outside my system. You have failed! Oh, pale Carpenter, look around you. No such people exist! Your hopes for a new citizenship, for something besides civilization—some kind of new nation outside my system—are dashed. You dreamed for a new species inhabiting a new way of life that would replace me. That dream dies here. Now, drink the cup! I shall take my glistening beauty and wrap it as a shroud around you and all the citizenry of earth! See what lies ahead for the planet you created: golden chains, a prison with bejeweled cells, and diamond-studded prison walls! No one can flee my pyramid of systems. There will be no community of the redeemed in which to find refuge."

At last I replied. "Tell me, World, who is your ruler? Who is the final lord?"

"Oh, with perverse joy I will gladly pronounce his name. Deceiver, the greatest of all deceivers. Oh, my beloved satanic one. He is head of all governments. He is ruler of all my systems."

"Bring him forth," I commanded.

I heard the smooth yet cackling voice of the most fallen of all fallen creatures.

"I am here, Carpenter. And I, too, have come to watch you die. I have come to seize your throne!"

I replied, "No! I ordered you here! Your pitiful powers end in the presence of my authority. You have come for me? Furthermore, great deceiver, there is a word I want you to utter."

"What word would that be, Son of God?"

"It is a simple term, but you cannot say it. Call me *Son* of Man."

There was only resounding silence.

"You know you cannot call me by this name, deceptive one.

"Long ago, in a garden, a man was sent to rule the earth. Not a king, not a god, but an ordinary man. It was his to bring you to an end."

"Yes, and I led that man away," came the nervous reply.

"None but a *man* can end your reign—and another man has come."

"True, Carpenter, but look around you: I have once again gained the upper hand. Today you will die as surely as that first man fell, no matter that you are Son of God!"

"Still you will not say it, will you, Lucifer! This creation belongs to a man, not to an angel, and certainly not to a *fallen* angel like you. You *cannot* call me Son of *Man*. A second man, a new kind of man, even a new species of man, has arrived on this planet to take his reign upon this earth. A man, born of a Jewish maiden, has come here to overthrow your usurping reign!"

Lucifer fell back in silence. Then, changing his demeanor, he cried out, "Today, God, I will kill you!"

"No, this man alone will choose his death and destroy you—and your dark kingdom."

"I will find a way to destroy you, Son of God."

"I, the Son of Man, have *found* a way to destroy you. The instant of your destruction will be here on this hill.

"There is another I now summon here, Lucifer. The one who is coming is one you know well.

"I call forth sin itself!"

Chapter 26

"I, SIN, HAVE also come to watch you die, but more than that. You are the only soul I have never touched. We not only meet this day, but it is I alone who will be your end. I have come to you, Carpenter, to have you work for me in this my hour. I have come to make you my employee."

"I have never worked for you," responded the Carpenter. "Nor did you come to me on your own. I called you here!"

"True, true," screeched Sin, "but this day you will work for me. And I will pay you well; I will pay you so very well," shrilled Sin hysterically.

With a voice almost swooning with delight, Sin continued, "What do I pay? What are the wages? Oh, the wage I pay is so glorious. I do not pay in silver, nor do I pay in gold or diamonds.

"I pay in *death*," continued an enraptured Sin.

"All have worked for me except you. All! And I have paid them all the same wage. At last, even you will work for me, even this hour!" came Sin's voice, overburdened with delight.

"But until I work for you, you cannot bring death to me, can you, Sin?"

Sin, like Lucifer, fell silent.

"There will be found a way, and it will be today!" hissed Sin. "You will sin. Then shall I bring death to you and pay your wage in full."

"No, I will not deal with you in matters of sins. If I am to deal with you at all, it will not be with some sin, but it will be with all sin."

There came another scream of hysteric delight. "Yes! Oh, yes! Then do so. Do so now, Carpenter. Swear it to me. Tell me you will deal with me who is *all sin*. All the sin of all mankind. All sin there has ever been before or after—on the earth, beneath the earth, above the earth, above the skies, and in all the realms of all the principalities and powers. I will gladly give up all my prey in order to see you becoming me!"

"Hear me now, Sin, Lucifer, World. This day I have dealt with the Hebrews. This day I have dealt with the *heathen*. Now it is time for you to be dealt with by me, you citizens of darkness, you infernal clan."

The one who now stood before me was sin incarnate. I commanded, "You, the source of all iniquity, stand here and listen to me."

Again the scream of delight.

"Yes," replied Sin, "We, the enemies of God, await your end! Behold all who have again thwarted the Carpenter's purpose!"

I then addressed the fallen angel. "Draw near, Lucifer. Long ago you were my servant. Now, you are but the captain of the damned, and you wait for naught but for your own damnation. Liar of liars, prince of all darkness, ruler of the world's system, head of all religion, government, science, fashion, education, and commerce—you have boasted that you brought down *man*. Not so, for it is a man who commanded you here. You shall be found out to be the ruler of nothing.

"World, approach me. You are the one who brings man into his first snares. You are the forger of men's bonds. Bring here your chains. Before I breathe my last, it will be chains that bind you.

"Come to my Cross. Each of you has announced that you have thwarted my purpose. You are congregated here to sing your discordant song of victory and to dance upon my grave.

"Behold, I call yet another to come and stand before my Cross."

Lucifer turned and then began to laugh.

"Pitiful Galilean!" Lucifer replied with biting sarcasm, "You would call forth your greatest failure! You would bring here your failed attempt at man's salvation. Never has there been such failure! You would call to this place your efforts to bring redemption to mankind. Your failed attempt at rescuing man only brought forth man's worst frustrations. Let the last thing you ever see, Carpenter, be *your* tragic endeavor to eradicate the sins of mankind."

Ignoring the torrents of the prince of this world, I called out, "Come forth, Law!

"Law, take your place before my Cross."

Chapter 27

Law appeared.

Law—stern, cold and inflexible—made its way before my Cross.

But it was World who spoke next: "Men tried so hard to live up to your demands, Law, and most were not only defeated, but also discouraged. In their defeat they found comfort in me, the World System!"

I said, "Law, come bring me your endless list of rules which men are to do or not to do."

World sneered, "The harder they tried to do those good deeds, the more they were drawn to do the opposite."

"Ten things not to do," scoffed Lucifer. He added in mock surprise, "No, not ten! *Six hundred and thirteen* things a man must or must not ever do! And, let us not forget moons, months, days, seasons, and Sabbath. All were needed for man's salvation."

"Yes," proudly interrupted Sin, "but the strength of sins was so much greater than all those demands."

Having had their say, I reminded them of one thing of which they had not spoken. "You enemies of Adam's race, you forgot the lamb!"

Lucifer fell quiet. I continued, "Even death could not press beyond the blood of the lamb placed upon the doorpost."

"True, Carpenter," trumpeted Sin, "but do not forget that my child, my *kin*, will arrive here in a moment. Then shall we see who has final victory. Like all lambs before you, Carpenter, you, too, will die when Death arrives! Then shall all your feeble efforts die with you."

Chapter 28

"I HAVE A question to ask you whom I have summoned here: Has it passed your notice who you are?"

"We are your enemies," announced Sin. "*And* we are here to watch you die."

"I have no enemies here," I responded.

Those present at my Cross did not grasp what I said to them.

"Those of you who are here have never been *my* enemies. You are the enemies of *mankind*. You are those who have distracted the race of Adam. *Never* for a *moment* have any of you ever been my enemy!"

"But you *do* have an enemy," corrected Sin.

With that, Sin sensed that some awful creature was drawing near.

"Yes, you do have an enemy, Carpenter, and he approaches even now! Death is near!"

"Yes," I replied, "death is very near."

"Come, Death!" cried Sin. He bellowed, "Here comes one who *can* kill God!

Lucifer spoke: "Even as the life seeps out of you, Son of God, there comes one to steal your last breath. Then you will be snuffed out forever. Oh, what a blessed moment," smacked Lucifer. "Then there will be no divinity," he continued. "The universe will be void of all but lower life-forms and highest death. Death, in triumph over life. Death shall reign supreme."

"Son of God," continued my tormentors, "Your creation, both seen and unseen, shall fall into Death's eternal coffin and under his rule."

"You know not all things," I replied. "When Death arrives, I have a challenge to lay before him."

As I spoke these words, the unseen world began to fade. I was once more in the realm of space and time.

Chapter 29

"LORD."

It was the thief.

His face was swollen, his eyes dark and vision blurred, every breath a struggle. I was certain that these would be among the last words the thief would be able to utter.

My time was also very short. I could smell the stench of approaching death.

I heard a tone in the voice of this thief I had not heard before, though it was but one single word, Lord.

"Lord, have we met before?" he asked.

"Perhaps."

"Then when?"

"Before the beginning. Or perhaps at the end. Or after the end. I walk the corridors of space and time, transcendent over past or future, this realm or the other. I knew you before time existed, I knew you before I created, even before I said 'Let there be light.' "

The old thief shook his head, "I have no idea of what you speak, but I know that no one else has spoken as you do.

"I ask one thing of you, Lord: Is it possible, in that moment of your triumph when you enter into your kingdom, is it possible that you might...*rem*ember me?"

"Remember you?" I replied. "How can I possibly forget you? You are the first of my salvation. You are my first conquest over death. You, above all others, are the first evidence of my redemption. How can I forget you? There is a book called the Book of Life. Your name has been written therein, long, long ago."

The thief understood nothing, but in a few moments, he would know everything. He would know even as he was known.

"Lord, I know nothing of your teachings. I know nothing concerning your demands. Nor can I as much as move. There is no way I can serve you. What is there that I can do?"

"There is but one demand, and you have already met it. You have learned to call me *Lord*. I will, therefore, enter your innermost being and dwell with you for all eternity. That is quite enough for you to know."

"Even though I have no knowledge of what you speak, Lord, something in me also says it is enough. May I ask my question again? Will you please remember me?"

I struggled to find one last, strong breath.

"Before this day is over, you will be with me in paradise."

"How can that be?"

"It can be because I chose you long before there was anything, including *nothingness*. And the first name ever written in the Book of Life was penned by me. And, you, thief—it was *your* name that was first written therein.

"Now close your eyes, redeemed one. When you open them again, open them in paradise.

"Now it is time."

The scene on the hill began to change.

"It is now time for me to summon even Death."

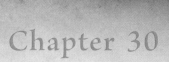

Chapter 30

"DEATH, YOUR HOUR has arrived," I whispered.

"Come forth from the netherworld. Let us speak to one another, Death, before we both die."

"He comes! He comes! My child comes," screeched Sin. "Come to me my son, your mother calls. Come from the east, gathering all that is filth. Come from the west and gather all that is abomination. From the north gather all that is wicked. And from the south gather together here all that is evil. Come from the depths of the seas, from places long since forgotten. Come from places that have ceased to be. Come, you infernal horde. Come from the deepest cesspools of depravity and wantonness. Gather all the dregs of hell, all that is unnatural. Bring together all blasphemies of time and eternity."

With bloated arrogance Sin declared, "I smell his rotting fetor. There is no one like him—he is the greatest of all gods! He is my forever companion."

Worldliness turned its face in shame. The principalities, the damned demons, and the unclean spirits gasped for breath.

Never before had *all* sin been confined to such a small space. The very earth shook in uncertain horror. Sun and stars closed their eyes. Jerusalem shook in terror, as did all the pilgrims of the Passover.

Even Lucifer looked away.

From this unholy scene emerged the seraphimic monstrosity—Death!

"There is none so proud as you, oh Death. Come and tell us of your greatness," I coaxed.

"Let them see your fare," exclaimed Sin, so sickly proud of her son.

"He is god of all gods. Listen to him, let him tell you that which is true."

Death began his soliloquy: "Ahh, we meet again, one who is called God."

Chapter 31

"I CAME FORTH from the bowels of my mother, Sin, when I first met you face to face at the rebellion in the other realm. Then, upon the night of the Passover, you denied me my rightful spoils. I swore that night I would someday have you as my prey.

"Tragic, Nazarene, that there are but two gods left. I am one, and the other is dying on a tree. You have never known death, Son of God. I have never known life. I am the negation of all that you are. The God who lives and the god who cannot live spend our last moments together. Then silence! Then it will be I alone!"

Death raised his undefeated claws and screamed, "At last, upon this hill, you are mine!

"I, Death, extinguish the hate in every man's heart.

"I end man's doubts and questions, forever.

"I am the one whom the aged embrace with joy.

"I end all pain.

"I, and I alone, release all suffering.

"Let me tell you why it is that I alone should be god!

"I finish all wars.

"I end all negotiations.

"You, dying Galilean have brought light into creation.

"I brought darkness that never ends.

"No one has ever won an argument with me.

"You brought life to a few.

"I have brought an end to all.

"The most powerful have fought and lost.

"There are no exceptions.

"I make equal all men.

"There are no great or small.

"You have raised one, yea, two, perhaps three, from the grave.

"I have plunged myriads upon myriads into the grave.

"Not one escaped my smothering hands.

"How strong is love?

"I am stronger still.

"In my castle, life and love will be forgotten.

"Divinity will be annihilated.

"Never will such seed ever grow again."

Death continued roaring his self-praises.

"Can you not see that I only am worthy to be called god?

"You are Creator.

"Who is greater, he who creates or he who obliterates?

"Then, of *my* kingdom there shall be no end.

"Witness now the end of all you have done.

"Within this hour there shall be but one god.

"The other shall be forever dead.

"Look around you, Carpenter. All sin is embodied here.

"*Now* drink the cup.

"Drink all the dregs.

"You who once were called Lord.

"Let all the filth of sin become yours.

"Absorb all iniquity.

"Know that as you do, *that* will be your final draught.

"In that instant shall I come!

"I will wrap you in my embrace.

"There shall I hold you so tightly that your last breath will also be the last breath of the universe.

"Then shall I crown myself god, while dancing upon your tomb.

"None will be left alive except the ones who *cannot* live. The one who is forever dead shall rule all things. I shall establish my kingdom in a place where all citizens are breathless."

Sin was in ecstasy while Death was intoxicated with his own pride.

"Carpenter, you have declared you have but one enemy, that all others are but the adversaries of mankind. It is true! They have been victorious only over the sons of Adam. But now behold me, your enemy. I am your victor!"

"Death, are you finished with your self-exaltation?" I asked.

Chapter 32

"SERAPHAMIC RULER OF the netherworld, you are my equal? So you say.

"You can kill even God? So you say.

"Of this one thing you are correct: *This* is the final battle.

"Life versus death."

"Death versus no less than eternal *life,*" gloated Death. "Our final battle, if I win, will be the eradication of the life of God."

"Or should you lose, the eradication of death!" I added.

"It shall never be," bellowed Death. "I will kill divine life and it shall never be known again."

"So shall it be—or so you say," I replied.

At that moment the cup appeared.

Even Death could not look upon the spewing venom of its contents.

Out of his mind with perverse joy, Death began to chant.

"My hour, my hour.

"At last, my hour.

"The last hour ever there shall be."

"Death, I ask if you can kill me."

"Yes, yes," he frothed with insane delight. "I can. I can!"

"Can you kill me *without* the cup?"

Death whimpered and fell silent.

"Then never forget, it is by my will alone that the cup is here."

At that moment the cup was poised to pour its contents into me. The rage of all sin began to fill every cell in my body. My heart, then my mind, began to falter. I, who had never sinned, who was unacquainted with transgressions, was suddenly becoming one with sin.

My end was at hand. I had not only taken sin into me. I was becoming its incarnation. I knew my life could not long endure.

When I cried out in my delusion, Death knew this was his moment. Death then bellowed with fiendish glee and plunged toward me. My body and soul were ablaze with what was now permeating my all. With a body on fire, I heard myself cry out, "I thirst!"

One of the soldiers grabbed a sponge and, in the only act of mercy of that day, he plunged the sponge into the sour wine, looking as he did it for some way to raise it to my mouth.

That moment filled my last sight.

John had cautiously made his way to the hill and was standing next to my mother.

"John, this is *your* mother now.

"Mother, this is now your son."

My sight failed me. I was blinded by the contents within my soul. In a moment I would not be human.

I...would...be...sin!

Chapter 33

"I LIVED BEFORE you ever existed," I said to Death as he squeezed me in his clutches. "Poor Death, there are things that took place before you existed of which you know nothing."

"It matters not," Death vaunted.

"It matters *all*," I replied.

In that final moment I commanded those who were present from the unseen realm: "Step forth, World System. Come into my very being.

"You, World, shall die with me!

"Lucifer, principalities and powers, and all whom you head, come into me.

"Law, you have been fulfilled, now come into my bosom.

"Adam's race, all that was touched by the Fall, and creation itself, come into me and be one with me!

"Death, be my servant: Put to death all that is now one with me.

"Come, religion! That which strives to be good but is ever failing, come.

"Death, take religion, the old man, and the self nature and make them your prey.

"Die upon my Cross. Come, all of you, die in me! You have now encountered the most destructive power in creation—my Cross!

"Put me to death, I command you. Death, look at me: I am become the Fall.

"*All that is created* is crucified with me.

"Oh, but there is one left!

"Death, as you take the last breath from me, I have a surprise for you.

"Death, *you* are now mine!" I cried out triumphantly.

Chapter 34

As Death wrapped himself about me, to snuff out the last ember of my life, I whispered to Death, "*You* are not death. Is there not one greater than you?"

"None," frothed Death.

"Is there not one who can put Death to death?"

"There is no such a one!" screamed Death.

"Not true," I replied. "You have for so long called yourself Death, but I was here long before you. I tell you now what you did not know then. I am disguised. You, Death, are but a shadow. You are not death at all. You are but a picture of me. No, Death, you are not death at all. I am life, it is true, but I also am the one who is true death. And at this last moment, I am death to you.

"Oh, Death, be now surprised. One is greater than all your vaunted claims. The one who can kill Death is death indeed. Today I kill you, Death. You thought you came for me, but it is I who came for you!

"Then, when Death be dead, then shall Sin also be dead, along with the principalities, the world, Adam's race, and the law. As Death dies, the law will be forever dead. When Death is dead, creation meets its end. And if Death be dead, then who shall hold the graves? There *will be* life for all who were once your prey.

"Death, hear me, there will be only one who inhabits the domain of the dead! That shall be you."

Death began to feel his power draining away. His eyes blazed in horror.

"I have crucified the world, I have crucified Sin, I have crucified Law, I have crucified the race of Adam, I have crucified creation, and I have crucified all else that has this hour entered into me."

Death cried, "I take comfort in this: I am also killing the Galilean. That is satisfaction enough for me. Let me end, here and now, but Carpenter, you shall lie in the grave beside me."

Death screamed and then screamed again as he sank into his grave. His last desperate utterance: "If I can hold you for three days, Carpenter, then will I hold you forever."

While everything I am that was not sin had fled from me, I cried out.

*Eloi, Eloi, lema sa*bachthani.

A bystander thought I was calling for Elijah.

The soldier had found the hyssop branch and was about to lift the sponge to my lips.

"Hold," someone said. "Let us see if Elijah will come and save him."

One last scene passed before me. I watched all creation and all within it die upon my Cross, and then I heard the voice of my Father, "Well done, my dear and faithful Son."

Hearing my Father's words, I cried out,

*It...is...*finished!

In the last second of life, I released my divinity to the Father.

Father, into your hands I entrust my spirit.

Chapter 35

THE CURTAIN TO the entrance of the Holy of Holies ripped open while splintering wood crashed upon the floor below.

Instantly the great and foreboding cloud that had gathered around Golgotha disappeared.

For the first time, the Passover was spent in chaos. Terrified priests attempted to find some way to cover the entrance into the Holy of Holies, yelling all the while, "Do not look upon the Holy of Holies!"

When told the door between man and the holiest place on earth was visible to ordinary people, Caiaphas tried to hide his panic.

At that same moment in heavenly places, the fierce cherubim with their ever-circling swords of fire (which had guarded the door between the two realms since the Fall) fled in terror because the door suddenly disappeared.

Not since Adam of earth and God of heaven walked in the garden had there been commerce between these two realms.

Angels, as terrified as the cherubim, fled that empty place where once had been the guarded door. Finally, when curiosity overcame them, the angels cautiously crept back to that place which had so long been sealed.

Chapter 36

IT WAS THREE o'clock in the afternoon.

I had been on the Cross for six hours.

Those executed by the cross never died in so short a time, as the point of crucifixion was to exhibit a long, merciless death.

Unsure that one could be dead so soon, the soldier raised a spear and pierced my side.

I was pierced in the same place where I long ago had opened Adam's side to bring forth his bride. The second man to be the head of a new race also had a woman inside him. In a few days, divine woman would come forth out of me.

As the soldier removed the spear from my side, first water flowed out of my side, then blood—thus fulfilling what I had told Zechariah.

With evening approaching—the hour of the Passover ritual—the Roman soldiers took iron rods and beat the legs of the two (very alive) thieves until their legs broke. A moment later both men died of suffocation. Because I was dead and proven to be dead, my legs remained unbroken, thus fulfilling my prophecy that none of my bones would be broken.

At last it was all over, but who would come for my body? As far as the Romans cared, my body was now meat for vultures.

My mother had kept a vigil, along with Mary her sister and Mary Magdalene.

Someone from the Sanhedrin, with newfound courage and faith, was about to lay claim to my body.

Chapter 37

ALTHOUGH THE PASSOVER was approaching, one of the men of the Sanhedrin had come to the hill to inquire about my body. It was Joseph from the nearby town of Arimathea. He dared not come too close to the dead, but he did ask the soldiers how he could go about removing my remains.

"Only Pilate can do that," replied one of the guards defiantly.

Joseph, a good and kind man, not present at my trial, nerved himself, went to see Pilate, and asked for my body. When Pilate heard that I was already dead, he did not believe it.

One of the guards assured him, "Sir, his side was pierced; he is dead. I was there."

With that word, Pilate gave Joseph permission to remove my body.

Soon another member of the Sanhedrin, a man named Nicodemus, joined Joseph and his servants. With time running out, they rushed to Golgotha to claim my body.

Brutally a guard ripped out the spike in my legs. Then, mounting the tree, guards cut the ropes holding my body to the crossbeam. My lifeless body fell to the ground.

Meekly and remorsefully, Nicodemus and Joseph, along with their servants, placed my naked body upon a long, white, linen sheath that covered my entire body.

Some years earlier, Joseph had purchased a tomb for himself and his family, one never before used. The tomb was near both Gethsemane and the place where I was crucified.

With the Passover only moments away, the servants rushed to Joseph's tomb and there left my body, along with seventy-five pounds of aloes and spices.

Just a short distance behind these men was my mother, wanting to be certain that she would know where I was laid. With my mother were Mary Magdalene and Mary the mother of James the younger and of Joseph.

Before departing, Joseph of Arimathea had his servants roll a huge stone across the entrance to my tomb.

No one in the entire universe could have grasped what lay in that tomb that evening.

Creation itself was in that tomb awaiting the birth of a new creation. That new creation would not take seven days, but rather just three, and its beginning would be from this very tomb. That new creation would be born instantly in a burst of light and power.

All the power of darkness, World, Sin, and Law were in that tomb. So also the Jewish race, the Gentiles, all the race of mankind. But most important of all, Death lay there, still and silent.

All were awaiting—

Awaiting their triumph or mine.

Would it be the powers of darkness which would arise? Or perhaps the all-consuming victory of Death, with the end of life forevermore?

Or?

Was it possible that nothing at all would come forth?

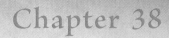

Chapter 38

"It has only been seconds as men count time, and already so much is changing."

"I cannot but wonder," mused one of the angels, "does the disappearance of the door mean that we will be able to go back and forth to earth as we once did with Adam?"

"Or more," asked another, "shall we see mortal beings setting foot in the realm of the spirituals?"

"I could not so imagine," replied one of the angels.

"Perhaps you are correct," agreed another.

There was a pause. All the angels looked toward the missing door and on to earth.

One startled angel blinked and asked, "Pray tell what is that I see? Whatever it is, it seems to have only this moment appeared. It seems to be coming this way."

"Forbid that fallen man should gain entrance to the habitat of the heavenlies!" exclaimed a rather concerned angel. "But what is that?"

"I have no idea," responded another angel.

"Could it be an angel of some kind we have never known?"

"No, it is far, far too bright to be an angel."

"Perhaps one of the vanished cherubim?"

"No, too bright even for that. Besides, cherubim are fierce. This appears to be trying to express some kind of overwhelming joy. It is not a cherub."

"It cannot be a human, can it?"

"Of course not! Fallen men are not allowed in the realm of things spiritual under any conditions. Well, whatever it is, it is coming this way."

"Then we perhaps should prepare to make flight."

"Why?"

"Because! Whatever it is, so bright, so holy, we may not have a right to live in its presence."

"Well, whatever it is, it is really making a great deal of noise."

"Quickly, who else has ever been in our realm before?"

"Well there was Enoch."

"Yes, and who else?"

"Moses looked upon our realm, but he did not come in."

"And then there was that visit by Isaiah."

"Yes, but he only stood at the edge of the Holy of Holies."

"Elijah."

"No, Elijah saw a host of angels girded for battle, but he did not come in."

"Anyone else?"

"Solomon saw our realm. David also glanced at it."

"But none just walked in?"

"Not as far as I can remember."

"Look at this one, he is most definitely on his way *here*, as he comes up the stairway of the clouds."

"He stumbles, runs, and stumbles again. Look, now he is jumping. He is definitely…coming in…here!"

"I have never seen such conduct," mused another of the angels.

"As I said, we may have to find some other place to live. For one thing, has there ever been such purity and holiness?"

By now the entire angelic host had moved to the unguarded entrance to heavenly places. "What light!" The angels were dumfounded with awe at the one approaching.

"He is transparent," called one of the angels. "I think that he can see both realms."

"I think he belongs to both realms."

"That is not possible."

"No, at least it was not previously possible."

"There is no doubt the one coming this way *thinks* he has a right to be here."

"What light," repeated one of the angels.

"I believe he can see us!"

"Is that possible? After all, we are invisible."

"I thought something like this would happen if the wall between the two realms disappeared—and it has."

"I miss having that door," said one very troubled angel.

"I do not like this vast, unguarded space," agreed another.

"Can you hear him? I believe he is speaking to us."

"Should not at least one of us draw a sword?"

"Pray tell what good that would do," declared another.

"Is this the end?"

"It appears to be more like the beginning. His light is growing brighter."

The angels began shielding their eyes.

Chapter 39

"ARE ALL OF you angels?" he asked.

"It is speaking to us!" exclaimed one of the angels.

"Am I an angel?"

The approaching creature paused and slowly looked around. "No, I guess I am not an angel. I think I used to be a human being. But oh, look at me!"

"I have never seen such innocence, purity, and perfection," whispered one of the angels. "He does not seem to be aware of how beautiful he is or how bright his light is."

"Where am I? What am I doing here? Who are you? Please, pray tell, what am I?"

"Dare we speak to him?" asked another of the angels.

"You have never seen anything like me, have you?"

"You are the first," stammered one of the angels, finally, "but...I have an idea you will not be the last. As to who you are...I would be pleased to tell you, but I do not know who or what you are."

"He told me that I would be here today. Is this today?"

The mouths of the angels fell open.

One said, "At last we know *who* you are!"

Another said, "That is not possible. After all, remember what he was: He was an old thief. That old, cheating, lying thief."

"Now I remember!" exclaimed the thief. "And, oh, oh, oh! *He* remembered me!

"We know who you are now, dear one. But we are a little surprised, considering what you were this evening."

"I am a thief. Or was. What am I now?

"You are the *first of the r*edeemed."

"You are the handiwork of Christ's redemption."

"That is what I am!" exclaimed the former thief.

"I have another question. Am I as beautiful as I think I am?"

"Even more so," replied the angels as one.

"Am I as bright as you are?" he inquired again.

"No. More so. Much more! We have *never* been that bright."

"Never before have I been able to see places which *cannot* be seen," observed the thief in wonderment. "Are you sure I am the only one of my kind?"

"Yes," answered one of the angels. "But we expect many more of your kind."

"You are the first of your species," another angel informed him.

"I think I died," said the thief. "I was on a cross just a few moments ago. Now look at me! Am I in...in...paradise?"

"This is at *least* paradise," replied the angel, "and perhaps it will be even more. We will know in three days. In fact, with your arrival, we are sure this will be much more than paradise—in three days."

At those words, this child of God grabbed one of the terrified angels, embraced him, and began to dance.

"Angels do not dance," observed one of the heavenly host gruffly.

"We do now," smiled another.

"I do not know who I am. I know not where I am. I do not know what I am, but I sense I am not what I used to be—*and* that I am wonderful and beautiful," he shouted.

Suddenly he paused. "The one dying next to me said that I would be with him in paradise, but he also mentioned something to me about a book. A Book of Life. Is there something called the Book of Life? Oh, also, there was something about being known even as I am known."

With that the angels rushed to the Book of Life. Just as they had expected, the very first name written in the Book was that of the thief.

The angels began to shout praises, joined by peals of laughter. They burst into a crescendo of song as rarely known before.

"I am the first of what?" he asked.

"You are the first of those for whom we have waited throughout the ages. We have long waited for this day to arrive."

"One last question: You are called *angels*. What am I called?" he asked.

"You are called a *h*oly one."

Chapter 40

IS THAT THE sun coming up? It is just now breaking over the ridge of the mountains. I feel the tremors of an earthquake.

This must be Sunday morning!

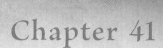

Chapter 41

My mother, Mary, had spent a terrible night filled with images of my last moments of life, of my hasty burial, and of the huge stone that had been rolled in front of the entrance to my tomb.

"Saturday was the strangest of days," she observed to her friends. Mary Magdalene had described it best: "It is as though the universe has come to a halt, with everything in creation waiting for something to happen."

Saturday night would be as fitful as Friday. Sadness and helplessness had engulfed all my followers. But for Mary, for the Magdalene, and for the other women, all their thoughts centered around the huge stone.

Nicodemus and Joseph of Arimathea had warned the women, "By no means should you come back to the tomb, not until Sunday."

Yet for Mary Magdalene, to return to that tomb was the only purpose she still had in life. Like the other women who had witnessed my body being laid into the grave, she had watched as a large group of very strong men rolled the circular stone into place. The women had seen the stone fall into a hewn notch, depriving anyone of access to the inner room, and thereby hopelessly sealing his body. All agreed, "The rock is now unmovable." It would take a multitude of men to budge that stone. And so they waited, watched, and wondered.

(As to the eleven, they were all in hiding. Where? No one knew except that they were somewhere in the city. And while in hiding, those eleven men were so stunned that they could hardly find their speech.)

And there was another problem. The Jewish leaders had gone to Pilate and asked the Romans to post soldiers in front of the tomb to guard it day and night. The Roman soldiers enjoyed frightening people by brandishing their swords, and should anyone venture to approach the tomb, the soldiers would give no quarter to the curious. Until these guards departed, it was a certainty no one would dare approach my tomb. Nor would a guard ever dare fall asleep during his watch. To do that would mean certain death. A guard found sleeping would be immediately set on fire and stabbed to death.

An unmovable stone and a platoon of well-trained soldiers had removed all hope for a brokenhearted woman to tend to my lifeless body.

The night's wait proved too much for Mary Magdalene. She determined that, regardless of the risk, she would go to my tomb and there keep her vigil.

She passed Gethsemane, the place of the crucifixion, and from there ran quickly on to Joseph's tomb. There she waited for a morning that seemed to refuse to come.

While the soldiers stood guard—and while Mary Magdalene made her way through the streets of Jerusalem—none could have imagined what was beginning to take place beneath the surface of my tomb, far below in the netherworld.

Death was dead, but its clutch upon me was unbreakable. It would take a power the likes of which has never been known to free me of death's cold hand. Not even the power which I unleashed at creation could triumph over this enemy of God.

Others had been raised from the dead, only to die again. If I, the Son of Man, was to be raised from the dead, it would be a resurrection once and forevermore. Then would all the work of death be doomed—and doomed forever.

There are things which had been reckoned as having life everlasting but were not everlasting because they were now in my tomb. Sin was once forever, but now it was forever in its grave. The Hebrews had thought that the sacred law had been established forever, yet the law lay quietly in its coffin, never to hold sway on men again. Then there was the world system, which had been born at the time of the Fall and had grown to encompass the planet. But that system died when I died. Also in my tomb, the entire race of Adam lay cold and dead. Things within the unseen realm had assumed the fallen human race would go on until the last child was born.

As to the prince of darkness, he, like the others, had had *everlasting life,* but my Cross had stolen such life from him.

In the eyes of God, all these which men had reckoned as everlasting were now everlastingly dead. Men may not comprehend the death of death, the end of sin, the destruction of the world system, the annihilation of the entire race of mankind, or the nullification of the kingdom of darkness, but in the eyes of God—and His view is the only view that counts—all of these were now in the tomb with me.

Only one question remained.

Could the Son of Man be raised from the dead? Could an entire species vanish and a new species come forth in its place?

Did such power exist?

That was, of course, impossible. Creation had been completed in seven days. God would not create again. But the Father knew something no others knew. He had reserved the right to bring forth that which was not *created*—rather, that which was uncreated—His own divine life! He would bring forth life that was *not* created!

So it was, in the darkest hour of Saturday, there gathered beneath me a power greater than that which had

been released by me when I created the galaxies, the earth, and man.

The gathering together into one place of such power caused the very earth to tremble. From the smallest atom to the grandest galaxy, things both seen and unseen began to lose their established ways. In the throes of such a cataclysm, creation itself began to groan while terror spread its wings across the very ends of the universe.

Chapter 42

DURING ALL THIS tempest I lay cold and breathless, dead as any creature who had ever died. Nor was Death's furious grip likely to release its prey. Was Death's power as great as the power of the Eternal Spirit?

And so began the duel.

Death versus Life. Life over Death.

Chapter 43

ANGELS, SENSING THE plaintive cry of planets, orbs, and spheres, tried to discern the origin of the cosmic disturbance.

Eventually the heavenly host realized there was no particular direction in which to take flight, for from molecules to galaxies all things were in uncertain turmoil.

"The conflict is somewhere beneath the earth, near Jerusalem," announced one of the angels.

As one, they now understood. "It is almost the third day." With that the entire angelic host moved—as it had three days earlier—to the hills of Jerusalem. There the anxious messengers of God took up an uneasy watch, knowing that the outcome of the ensuing battle would decide the fate not only of creation, but also of eternity.

Could the Eternal Spirit break Death's vice? Could the Eternal Spirit win over Death? Does that mean that eternal life—even the very life that God lives by, divine life—could become the life-source of man?

And there was more.

The Spirit was striving to impart eternal life to a new species of mankind, and that same Eternal Spirit was extinguishing the old creation. A new species could now live in utter freedom in a new creation.

The earthquake intensified, and some of the graves in Jerusalem ripped open. Places long forgotten, the burial place of Adam and Eve, shook in grand relief as all the descendants of the first family came to an everlasting end.

Still Death's hold would not relent.

The blazing light of Life spread beneath my tomb, so intense that angels, who can so clearly see the unseen, were certain that the brightness of the Eternal Spirit would set the entire planet aflame.

"Not since the Fall has creation known such throes," murmured an awe-stricken angel. "Shall God now annihilate this fallen realm? Or is something even more profound being done?"

The quakes intensified.

Jerusalem's hills began heaving stones into the air, fissures formed in the earth, buildings reeled. And in all of Israel graves were being denied their peace.

"Is it something of Death?" whispered one of the angels.

"Or perhaps something of Life," responded another.

As earth's spasms grew, so also the brightness grew. This was not the light of stars, nor of suns, nor of fire, but rather a brightness no angel had ever known nor beheld.

"This is God before he ever created us! This is God before there was anything. This is what God was like when He was the all!" exclaimed one of the angels breathlessly.

"Our eyes are seeing something that no created thing has ever before beheld," breathed another.

"This is the gathering together into one place of all there is of the Eternal Spirit," spoke another in hushed awe.

"He is here in a place so confined that..." Another angel broke in, "We are seeing the unleashed, unbridled, unhindered, limitless power of God...in just one place... beneath the tomb."

"Can this mean the power of Death is as great as the power of Life? We are witnessing the ultimate duel. No war ever fought can compare with this battle."

And still the raging turbulence of things seen and unseen continued to grow.

"I can feel the very anger of God. Life has such hatred for Death," choked another.

Realizing that the violence they were feeling was far greater in unseen realms than in the physical realm, a chorus of angels cried out, "The heavens are being rent asunder!"

The brightness of the light finally forced the angels to turn away. The entire heavenly host, with faces shielded in awe-smitten reverence, dropped to their knees. Quietly they began to weep. The light which had been emitting from beneath that tomb was now radiating through the angels. The light of the glory of the power had so enveloped everything that there was no room for anything save glory.

"Why has it not yet broken?" wondered one of the angels out loud. "The light so bright, the power so enormous, why is not Death yet swallowed up in Life?"

"This supernal display of the Spirit of life and power must end, or all that existed will be consumed."

Swallowed up in the life of my Father, Death's hold at last began to weaken.

Deep within the tomb something moved.

Chapter 44

FOR A MOMENT there was a burst of light such as no man, nor angel, nor pen could ever describe. For one brief, glorious moment the entire universe was enveloped in God.

Death was dissolving in the presence of glory.

In that same moment, Magdalene was moving toward the tomb, struggling to walk, as the earth continued to tremble. As she was thrown to the ground, she dropped her vases of precious ointments she had planned to use to embalm my body. They spilled on the ground and their oils sank into the troubled earth.

"Oh, my Lord!" cried the Magdalene, "You once delivered me from such bondage as womankind has ever known. If this be my hour, then I praise you for releasing me from the pain which is in my heart, for I have lost you, my Lord, my everything."

While I was still lost in the sleep of death, I suddenly felt! It was my hand that moved. Then my feet, with the wounds they bore. I had begun to move out of the deep tunnels of the netherworld.

My Spirit began to glow.

Then came a cry, a shout of triumph, a shout so great that even the discerning ears of angels could not comprehend its origin. As the cry beamed its way across the worlds, it finally came to be understood.

"It is *his* voice," they cried as one, "but the words, what are his words?"

I AM RISEN!

Then the waiting angels cried out with a shout as had never been heard before. It was a grand alleluia. But in that same triumphant moment the angels did something no mortal could ever understand. Each and every angel unsheathed his sword, and they all buried those swords in the soil of the hills of Jerusalem.

"He is victorious! The battle is over!"

As his shout of acclamation ascended across the galaxies, angels, fearing for their own well-being, covered their ears, yet continued their exultations.

"The hour of Jonah has been fulfilled!" they roared.

I stood!

With a joy that no man nor angel (but God alone) would ever know, I passed through my grave clothes. I folded the cloth from my head and laid it in the corner of the tomb. I raised my hands to the everlasting God, my Father, who was now proven to be Lord of All.

"Father, death and the grave are beneath your feet!"

I then threw back my head and cried out again.

I have risen!

I have risen!

I have risen!

I have risen from the dead!

"The enemies of man, the enemies of God are vanquished!" I exclaimed. "At last it is safe for the new species to come forth. There is nothing to hinder the new race."

The next moment was the most joyous moment I had ever lived! I touched my side!

I cried out with a voice that almost dissolved creation, "She is no longer inside me! I am no longer alone. Oh, Eternal Spirit! Oh, Father! You who have made me Lord of heaven and earth have given to me one who is spirit of my Spirit. Here is my grandest hour.

"I am no longer alone.

"*She* lives. Father, you have loosed her to the earth.

"She has no enemies, nor does she even know of their existence, for she walks in the new creation.

"She cannot see that which once was, for she is born after they have passed away.

"Just as my Father is not created, neither is she, for she is bone of my bone, flesh of my flesh, spirit of my spirit, eternal life of my eternal life.

"Father, you have brought her forth, the female of me."

Lest the very tomb itself should melt from my radiance, I walked to the entrance and passed through the stone door.

Having passed through the stone, I was greeted by angelic shouts and cries of ebullition as have never heretofore been heard. (And never will be again until the hour of my wedding.)

"She has come forth!" I cried. "This day I have fashioned neither stars, nor planets, nor orbs, but I have fashioned her out of my divine matter. My new creation is nothing less than my own species. As I am, so is she. Like me she is divine, yet human. She is my divinity, she is my humanity. She is my match. She is my substance. The shadow of oneness has passed away; the reality of oneness is here. This woman is of my own kind.

Having understood, the angelic host burst into what could only be described as delirium!

Chapter 45

THE EARTHQUAKE ENDED.

As she rose to her feet, Mary Magdalene looked around. There in the east she saw the first ray of the sun breaking over the hills.

"It is Monday morning. My Lord has been three days in the grave. *Three days*...has my Lord...been dead." This very thought turned her face into a river of tears. Mary then slipped to her knees, weeping uncontrollably.

She looked up with a start. "What was that? Some kind of shout?" she asked herself. "Some call of triumph? Was it a trumpet, perhaps? Never have I heard anything like it. Or did I not hear it at all? It seemed to...come from... *within* me. Whatever it was, it was beautiful, like the cry of thousands of angels."

Mary Magdalene stared at the broken vases and her failed attempt to preserve her Lord's body.

"I cannot even tend to your body. The oils are gone. Oh, dear God, I beg you, bring forth some miraculous way to preserve his body. Man cannot, but I know that you can."

Mary began making her way to what she did not know was empty at that moment—a very empty tomb.

Her thoughts turned toward the soldiers. She was certain they would draw their swords and then order her away. She felt certain she would hear one of them call out,

"So you are the one who comes to steal away the body of the carpenter?" She could even hear their scorn, "You are welcome to the body. All you have to do is roll away the stone."

It came about that as she neared the tomb, but without having yet seen it, the stone was in fact removed! And it had been moved for her.

With joy, two archangels had stepped forth and effortlessly rolled back the stone. It was now for the universe to see that the tomb was indeed empty.

Principalities did not see this hour, for it was not theirs to see.

Law did not see this hour, for it was not for Law to see.

Neither Sin nor Death saw this hour, for it was not theirs.

Neither was it for the race of Adam, for their hour had passed.

As the stone rolled back, the morning sunlight burst into the tomb. The angels lifted their hands and exclaimed,

"It is empty! There is no one here!"

As Mary Magdalene approached the tomb, she was overwhelmed by sorrow and brokenheartedness. She fell once more upon her knees and wept. "How shall we ever open the tomb?" she pleaded.

Then she looked toward the tomb and saw the stone had been rolled away! She rushed into the grave.

"They have stolen his body! They have stolen his body! Now I will never find him.

"No tomb in which to lay him. No ointments on him to pour. Oh, his body, vanished forever! Oh, where will I ever be able to go to again pour forth my love for him?"

With eyes swollen and with tears still falling copiously, she stepped out of the tomb. It was then that she heard a sound.

"The caretaker! The caretaker of Joseph of Arimaethea's garden. Perhaps he knows...perhaps he has seen something...perhaps he followed the soldiers who carried away my Lord's lifeless body.

"Oh gardener! Oh gardener! Please, please tell me, what have they done with the body of my Lord? Tell me, that I may go to him, wherever he may be."

It was the heart of this young girl to find my cold body and fall upon it again, to anoint me with her tears as she had done once before at a banquet I had attended.

She tried to wipe away her tears so she could more clearly see, and she waited to hear the voice of the caretaker.

With joy I smiled at one who had learned the simplest, yet greatest truth. It was out of this simple heart, out of this maiden, there had come the greatest, highest desire of God. That was, simply to be loved.

With all gentleness, I spoke one word.

"Mary."

The Magdalene whirled around. "Rabboni! Oh, my Rabboni, my Rabboni!"

In an instant she clutched me with such an embrace that I was fearful she would never let me go.

Mary Magdalene did the most glorious thing—the thing divinity has ever longed for. She loved me with all her heart, with all her mind, and with all her strength.

"Mary," I said, "you must let me go. It is time for me to ascend into the heavens. I am going there in triumph. The angels await me. It is the hour of my coronation. The seraphim are there. The cherubim are there. But most of all, my Father awaits me. I must go there, Mary, to take my place beside the throne of God."

I knelt down beside her and whispered, "And now Mary, I want you to do something for me. I want you to go and tell my brothers."

I looked into Mary's startled face. She exclaimed, "Your brothers! They are your followers, not your brothers."

"Mary, there is a new race on the earth. The old race of man is gone. You may not understand this, and you may not see it. But my Father sees it and so do I, and that is all that is important.

"Mary, you are now my sister. You are kin of my kin. You are kind of my kind. There is no difference now in our bloodline. I was once divine and became human. No creature such as that existed before I came here to earth. I was a totally new but singular species. Now all that has changed. Now my species has increased and will continue to increase. As surely as I am the Son of God and the Son of Man, you are my sister, a child of God. There now dwells within you that which is redeemed humanity, and there also now dwells in you my divinity. Yes, Mary, go tell those who are now my brothers. Tell them three words:

I have risen.

I have risen from the dead.

"Go quickly, Mary. I shall now ascend to my Father and your Father. But do not be troubled, for before the sun sets on this glorious day...

I shall *see* my brothers...

I shall *be with* my brothers...

I shall be *in* my brothers!"

God so loved the world

that He gave

His only begotten Son.

JOHN 3:16

Part 2

A BIBLICAL NARRATIVE OF THE CRUCIFIXION AND RESURRECTION

On the following pages is a blending of the four Gospels into one story that tells the crucifixion of Jesus Christ.

All four Gospels are included with nothing left out. The blended story is all scripture and a complete record of the day Christ was crucified, including dates and times.

The Betrayal

IT WAS TWO days before the Passover Festival. The Feast of Unleavened Bread, which begins the Passover celebration, was drawing near.

Jesus told his disciples, "The Passover celebration begins in two days, and Jesus the Son of Man will be betrayed and crucified."

At the same time the leading priests, teachers of the law, and other leaders were meeting at the residence of Caiaphas, the high priest, plotting Jesus' murder. They were still looking for an opportunity to capture him and put him to death. "But not during Passover," they said, "or there will be a riot"—a possibility they feared.

Then satan entered Judas Iscariot, who was one of Jesus' twelve disciples. Judas went over to the leading priests and captains of the temple guard to discuss the way to betray Jesus to them. The leading priests were delighted when they heard why he had come, and they promised him money. They gave him thirty pieces of silver. From that moment on, he began looking for the right time and place to betray Jesus so that they could arrest him quietly when the people were not nearby.

The Passover

April 3, AD 30

His disciples prepared to eat the Passover meal together with Jesus.

The evening of April 3, AD 30

Now the first day of the Feast of Unleavened Bread arrived, when the Passover lambs were sacrificed. So Jesus sent Peter and John ahead to Jerusalem and said, "Go and prepare the Passover meal, so we can eat together."

"Where do you want us to go to prepare for the supper?" they asked him.

"As soon as you go into the city," he told them, "a man carrying a pitcher of water will meet you. Follow him. At the house he enters, say to him, 'The teacher says, "My time has come and I will eat the Passover meal at your house. Where is the guest room where I can eat the Passover meal with my disciples?" ' He will take you upstairs to a large room that is already prepared. This will be the place; prepare the supper there."

The two disciples went on ahead to the city and found everything just as Jesus had said. So they did as Jesus told them and prepared the Passover meal there.

Before the Passover celebration, he knew that his hour had come to depart this world and return to his Father.

Having loved his own who were in the world, he loved them to the end. It was time for supper, and the devil had already put into the heart of Judas, the son of Simon Iscariot, to betray Jesus.

That evening at the proper time, the twelve disciples and Jesus were reclining at the table.

Jesus said, "I have looked forward to this hour, to eat this Passover meal with you before my suffering begins. For I tell you now that I shall never again eat it until it is fulfilled in the kingdom of God." Then he took a cup of wine, and when he had given thanks, he said, "Take this and share it. I will not drink of the fruit of the vine again until I drink it new with you when the kingdom of God has come."

Jesus knew that the Father had given all things into his hands and that he had come from God and was going back to God. He arose from the table, took off his robe and wrapped himself with a towel, and poured water into a basin. Then he began to wash the disciples' feet and to wipe their feet with the towel he had around him.

When Jesus came to Simon Peter, Peter said to him, "Lord! You would wash my feet?"

He answered, "You do not realize now what I am doing, but you will understand later."

"No," Peter protested, "you will never wash my feet!"

Jesus replied, "But if I do not wash you, you will not be part of me."

Simon Peter exclaimed, "Then, Lord, wash not only my feet, but also my hands and my head."

Jesus replied, "A man who has bathed is clean and only needs to wash his feet. You are clean, but not all of you are." Jesus knew who would betray him. That is what he meant when he said, "Not all of you are clean."

After washing their feet, he put on his robe and reclined again at the table. "Do you know what I have done to you? You call me Teacher and Lord; and you are right, because I am. And since I, your Lord and Teacher, have washed your feet, you ought to wash one another's feet. I have given you an example to follow. Do as I have done. Of a truth, a servant is not greater than his master. Nor is the one who is sent greater than the one who sent him. You know these things; you are blessed if you do them.

"I am not saying these things to all of you. I know the ones I have chosen, but the Scripture will be fulfilled:

> Even my close friend in whom I trusted,
> he who ATE my bread, has lifted up his
> heel against me.
>
> —PSALM 41:9

"I tell you this beforehand, so that when it happens you will believe I am He. Anyone who receives whomever I send receives me, and anyone who receives me receives the Father who sent me."

Now Jesus was troubled in spirit. As they were reclining at the table eating, he said, "Of a truth, one of you will betray me." Then the disciples, deeply grieved, began to say to him, "Surely not I, Lord?" They looked at one another and began to discuss among themselves which one of them would do such a thing.

Jesus responded, "It is one of you twelve. One is here eating with me who will betray me. I, the Son of Man, am going just as it is written of me, but woe to that man who betrays me. It would have been better if he had never been born!"

Judas, the betrayer, also asked, "Teacher, surely it is not I?" Jesus told him, "You have said it yourself."

One of his disciples, the one that he loved, was reclining on Jesus' chest. Peter motioned to the disciple for him to ask Jesus of whom he was speaking. Leaning back on Jesus' bosom, the disciple asked, "Lord, who is it?"

Jesus said, "It is the one whom I give the bread dipped in the bowl." And when he had dipped the bread, he gave it to Judas, son of Simon Iscariot. As soon as Judas had eaten the bread, satan entered into him. Then Jesus told him, "Hurry. Do what you will do." None of the others at the table knew what Jesus meant. Since Judas was the treasurer, some thought he was telling him to pay for the food or give money to the poor. Judas left at once, going out into the night.

As soon as Judas left the room, Jesus said, "The time has come for me, the Son of Man, to enter into my glory. God will bring me into my glory soon, and God will receive glory because of all that is happening to me."

As they were eating, Jesus took a loaf of bread and blessed it. Then he broke the bread in pieces and gave it to the disciples, saying, "Take this and eat, for this is my body given for you. Do this in remembrance of me."

After supper Jesus took a cup of wine and gave thanks. He gave it to them and said, "Each of you drink from it. This wine is a token of God's new covenant in my blood, which is poured out to forgive the sins of many. Mark my words—I solemnly tell you that I will not drink wine again until the day I drink it new with you in my Father's kingdom."

They began to argue among themselves as to who would be the greatest in the coming kingdom.

He said, "In this world kings lord it over their people, yet they are called benefactors. But among you, those who are the greatest should take the lowest place, and the leader should be a servant. The master is served by his servants. Is he not greater than his servants? But I am the one who serves you.

"You have stood by me in my time of trial. And just as my Father has given me a kingdom, I now grant you to eat and drink at my table in my kingdom. You will sit on thrones, judging the twelve tribes of Israel.

"Children, I will not be with you much longer. Then you will look for me, but you will not be able to find me, just as I also told the Jewish leaders.

"Now I am giving you a new commandment: Love each other. Just as I have loved you, love one another. By your love for one another, men will know that you are my disciples."

Peter replied, "Lord, where are you going?" He replied, "Where I go you cannot go with me now, but you will follow me later."

"But why can't I come now, Lord?" Peter asked. "I am ready to die for you."

Jesus answered, "Die for me? Before the rooster crows tomorrow morning you will deny three times that you know me."

His Promise

"DO NOT BE troubled. You have trusted God, now trust in me. In my Father's house there are many dwelling places. I am going to prepare a place for you. If this were not true, I would tell you. When everything is ready, I will come and receive you, so that you will always be with me where I am. And you know where I am and how to come there."

"No, we do not know, Lord," Thomas said. "We have not any idea where you are going, so how can we know the way?"

Jesus told him, "I am the way, the truth, and the life. No one can come to the Father except through me. If you had known who I am, then you would have known my Father. From now on you know him and have seen him!"

Philip said, "Lord, show us the Father and I will be satisfied."

Jesus replied, "Philip, do you not yet know who I am, even after all this time I have been with you? Anyone who has seen me has seen the Father! Why are you asking to see the Father? Do you not believe that I am in the Father and the Father is in me? The words I say are not my own; but my Father who lives in me. He does his work through me. Believe that I am in the Father and the Father is in me, or at least believe because of the works you have seen me do.

"Anyone who believes in me will do the same works I have done, and even greater works you will do because I am going to the Father. You can ask for anything in my name, and I will do it; this is because the work of the Son brings glory to the Father. Whatever you ask in my name I will do it. This is so that the Father will be glorified in the Son. Yes, ask anything in my name, and I will do it.

"If you love me, you will keep my commandments. I will ask the Father and he will give you another Comforter, who will never leave you. He is the Spirit of truth. The world cannot receive him because it does not see him or know him. But you do know him because he lives with you and will be in you. I will not abandon you—I will come to you.

"After a little while the world will no longer see me, but you will. Because I live, you will live also. When I am raised to life again, you will know that I am in my Father, and you are in me, and I am in you.

"Those who keep my commandments are the ones who love me. And those who love me will be loved by my Father, and I will love them. And I will reveal myself to them."

Judas (not Iscariot) said to him, "Lord, why are you going to reveal yourself only to us and not to the world?"

He answered, "All those who love me will keep my words. My Father will love them, and we will come to them and live with them. Anyone who does not love me does not keep my words. My words are not my own. The word which you hear is not mine, but the Father's who sent me.

"I am telling you these things now while I am still with you. But when the Father sends the Comforter in my name (the Holy Spirit), he will teach you everything and will remind you of everything I have told you.

"My peace I leave with you. And the peace I give is not the peace the world gives. So do not be troubled or afraid. As I told you, I am going away, and I will come to you. If you love me, rejoice because I go to the Father, who is greater than I am.

"I have told you before it happens, so that when it happens, you will believe.

"I do not have much more time to talk with you, because the ruler of this world is coming, and he has no part in me. I will do what the Father commanded me, so that the world will know that I love the Father.

"Come, let us go."

He Told His Disciples that He Loved Them

"I AM THE true Vine, and my Father is the Vinedresser. He cuts away every branch that does not produce fruit, and he prunes the branches that do bear fruit so they will produce even more. You have already been pruned because of the word I have spoken to you. Remain in me, and I will remain in you. A branch cannot produce fruit if it is severed from the vine, and neither can you unless you abide in me.

"I am the Vine; you are the branches. Those who remain in me, and I in them, will produce much fruit. Apart from me you can do nothing. Anyone who does not abide in me is thrown away like a useless branch and dries up. Such branches are gathered into a pile to be burned. But if you stay joined to me and my words live in you, you may ask what you wish to ask, and it will be done for you. My Father is glorified by this, that you bear much fruit and prove to be my disciples.

"I have loved you even as the Father has loved me. Remain in my love. When you obey me, you remain in my love, just as I obey my Father and remain in his love. I have told you these things so that my joy may be in you, and that your joy may be made full.

"This is my commandment: that you love each other just as I have loved you. The greatest love is to lay down one's life for his friends. You are my friends if you do what I ask of you. I no longer call you servants. A master does not confide in his servants. I have called you friends because I have told you everything the Father told me.

"You did not choose me. I chose you. I appointed you to go and produce fruit that will last, so that the Father will give you whatever you ask in my name.

"This is what I command you: that you love one another.

"When the world hates you, remember it hated me first. The world would love you if you belonged to it, but you do not belong to it. I chose you out of the world, and so the world hates you. Do you remember what I told you: 'A servant is not greater than his master.' Since they persecuted me, they will persecute you. If they heard my word, they will hear yours also. The people of the world will hate you because you belong to me, for they do not know God who sent me. They would not be guilty if I had not come and spoken to them, but now they have no excuse for their sin. Anyone who hates me hates my Father, too. If I had not done such miraculous signs among them that no one else could do, they would not be guilty. But they saw all that I did and yet hated me and also my Father. This has fulfilled what the Scriptures said:

They hated me without cause

—PSALMS 35:19; 69:4

"I will send you the Comforter—who is the Spirit of truth. He will come to you from the Father and will tell you of me. And you will also tell of me because you have been with me from the beginning.

"I have told you these things so that you will not stumble. You will be thrown out of the synagogue, and the time is coming when those who kill you will think they are doing God a service. This is because they have never known the Father or me. I tell you these things now so that when such an hour comes to you, you will remember I warned you. I did not tell you earlier because I was with you.

"But now I am going away to the One who sent me, and none of you has asked me where I am going. Because of these things I have told you, your hearts are filled with sorrow. But I tell you the truth—it is to your advantage that I go away, because if I do not, the Comforter will not come. If I do go away, he will come because I will send him to you. When he comes, he will convince the world of its sin, and of righteousness, and of judgment. The world's sin, not believing in me. Righteousness, because I go to the Father and you will no longer see me. Judgment, because the ruler of this world has been judged.

"I have many more things to say to you, but you cannot bear it now. When the Spirit of truth comes, he will guide you into all the truth. He will not speak his own ideas; he will speak what he hears. He will tell you all things. He will glorify me, for he will reveal to you what he receives from me.

"All that the Father has is mine; this is what I mean when I say that the Spirit will reveal whatever he receives from me.

"In a while I will be gone. You will not see me. Then, in another little while, you will see me again."

The disciples asked each other, "What does he mean when he says, 'You will not see me, and then you will see me'? And what does he mean when he says, 'I am going to the Father'? And what does he mean by 'a little while'? We do not know what he is talking about."

Jesus knew they wanted to ask him, and he said, "Are you asking yourselves what I meant? I said in just a little while I will be gone, and you will not see me; and again a little while and you will see me again. Of a truth, you will weep and mourn over what is going to happen to me, but the world will rejoice. You will grieve, but your grief will turn to joy. It will be like a woman in the pains of labor. When her child is born, she no longer remembers the anguish because of the joy that a child has been born into the world. You have sorrow now, but I will see you again; then your heart will rejoice, and no one will be able to rob you of your joy. At that time you will not need to question me about anything.

"Of a truth, if you ask the Father for anything in my name, he will give it to you. You have not asked in my name until now. Ask in my name and you will receive, and your joy will be made full.

"I have spoken of these things in stories, but the time is coming when this will not be necessary, and I will tell you plainly of the Father. Then you will ask in my name. I am not saying I will ask the Father on your behalf, for the Father himself loves you because you love me and believe that I came from the Father. I came from the Father into the world, and I will leave the world again and return to the Father."

Then his disciples said, "Finally you are speaking plainly and not in figures of speech. Now we understand that you know everything and no one should question you. By this we believe that you came from God."

Jesus answered them, "You now believe? The time is coming, and has already come, when you will be scattered, going each your own way, leaving me alone. Yet I am not alone, because the Father is with me.

"I have told you this so that you may have peace. In the world you have much tribulation and sorrow. Take courage; I have overcome the world."

Jesus asked, "When I sent you out to preach the Good News and you did not have any money or satchel or extra clothing, did you lack anything?"

"No," they replied.

"But now," Jesus said, "take your money and a sack. And if you do not have a sword, sell your clothes and buy one! The time has come for this prophecy about me to be fulfilled:

> He was numbered with transgressors.
> —ISAIAH 53:12

"Everything written about me by the prophets will come true."

"Lord," they replied, "we have two swords among us."

"That is enough," he replied.

Then they sang a hymn and went out to the Mount of Olives, as was Jesus' custom.

"Tonight all of you will desert me," he told them. "The Scriptures say,

God will strike the shepherd and the
sheep of the flock will scatter.

—ZECHARIAH 13:7

"But after I am raised from the dead I will go before you to Galilee and meet you there."

Peter declared, "Lord, even if everyone else deserts you, I never will."

But Jesus said, "Peter, this very night, before the rooster crows, you yourself will deny me three times. Simon, Simon, Satan has asked to have you, to sift you like wheat. But I have prayed for you, that your faith should not fail. So when you have repented and turned again, strengthen your brothers."

Peter said to me, "Lord, I am ready to go to prison with you and to die with you."

"Peter, of a truth, this very night, before the rooster crows, you will deny me three times."

"No!" Peter insisted. "Not even if I have to die with you! I will never deny you!" And all the others vowed the same.

Midnight—April 3, AD 30

After this, Jesus crossed the Kidron Valley to the Mount of Olives with his disciples and entered an olive grove named Gethsemane.

There he told them, "Sit here while I pray."

Jesus took Peter and Zebedee's two sons, James and John, and he began to be grieved and very distressed. He told them, "My soul is crushed with grief to the point of death, so stay here and watch with me. Pray that you will not be overcome by temptation."

Jesus went on a little farther (about a stone's throw) and knelt and fell face down on the ground. He prayed that, if it were possible, the awful hour awaiting him might pass from him. "Abba, Father," he prayed, "all things are possible for you. My Father! If you are willing, take this cup away from me. Yet I desire your will, not mine, to be done."

Then he returned to the disciples and found them asleep. He said to Peter, "Simon! Are you asleep? Could you not watch with me for even one hour? Keep watching and praying, so that you may not come into temptation. The spirit is willing, but the flesh is weak!"

He left them again a second time and prayed, saying the same words. "Father! If you are willing, take this cup away from me. Yet, if this cup cannot be removed unless I drink it, your will be done."

An angel from heaven then appeared and strengthened him. Being in agony, Jesus was praying very fervently, and his sweat fell to the ground like great drops of blood.

When he rose from prayer and returned to the disciples, he found them sleeping. They just could not keep their eyes open. "Why are you sleeping?" he asked. "Get up and pray that you may not enter into temptation." And they did not know how to reply.

Jesus went back to pray a third time, saying the same thing once more. Then he came to his disciples the third time, and said, "You are still sleeping? See, the hour has come. The Son of Man is being betrayed into the hands of sinners.

"Get up, let us be going. My betrayer is here!"

Betrayed with a Kiss

IMMEDIATELY, A MOB that was armed with swords and clubs arrived, with Judas leading them. He was one of Jesus' twelve disciples. Judas the betrayer knew this place, because Jesus had gone there many times with his disciples.

The mob had been sent out by chief priests, scribes, Pharisees (who were teachers of religious law), as well as elders of the people. The chief priests and Pharisees had given Judas a battalion of Roman soldiers and temple guards to accompany him. With blazing torches, lanterns, and weapons, they arrived at the olive grove.

Judas had given them a signal: "You will know which one to arrest when I go over and give him a kiss of greeting. Then take him away under guard."

As soon as they arrived, Judas came to Jesus. "Greetings, Teacher!" he said.

Jesus said, "Friend, do what you have come to do."

Judas then kissed him.

Jesus said, "Judas, you betray me, the Son of Man, with a kiss?"

Jesus realized all that was happening to him, and, stepping forward to meet the crowd, he asked, "Whom are you looking for?"

"Jesus of Nazareth," they answered.

"I am Jesus," he said.

Judas, his betrayer, was standing there with them.

As he said "I am Jesus," they drew back and fell to the ground!

Once more he asked them, "Whom are you looking for?" Again they replied, "Jesus the Nazarene."

"I told you that I am he," he said. "Since I am the one you want, let these go their way." Jesus did this to fulfill his own statement: "Of those whom you have given me, I have lost none."

Then the others seized Jesus.

When the disciples saw what was about to happen, they exclaimed, "Lord, should we strike with the sword?" Then Simon Peter pulled out a sword and cut off the right ear of Malchus, a servant of the high priest. But Jesus said, "Do not resist any further." He then touched the place where the man's ear had been and healed it.

Jesus then said to Peter, "Put your sword back into its sheath. Those who take up the sword will die by the sword. Do you not realize that I could ask my Father for thousands of angels to protect me, and he would send them instantly? But if I did, how would the Scriptures be fulfilled that say it must happen this way? Shall I not drink from the cup the Father has given me?"

Then Jesus said to the crowd and to those who led the mob, that is, the chief priests, officers of the temple, and the elders, "Am I so dangerous a criminal that you have come armed with swords and clubs to arrest me? Why did you not arrest me in the temple? I was there teaching every day. But this is your hour, and the power of darkness is yours. This is happening to fulfill the words of the prophets as recorded in the Scriptures."

Then all the disciples left Jesus and fled.

There was a young boy following him, wearing only a linen sheet over his body. When the mob tried to grab him, he pulled free of the linen sheet and escaped naked.

Jesus Was Tried by the Jews

Just before daylight, April 4, AD 30

So the soldiers, officers, and temple guards arrested Jesus and bound him. First they took him to Annas, for he was the father-in-law of Caiaphas, who was high priest that year.

(Caiaphas was the man who had told the other leaders, "Better that one should die for all.")

Inside, the high priest began asking about Jesus' followers and what Jesus had been teaching.

Jesus replied, "What I teach is widely known, because I have preached regularly in the synagogues and the temple where all the Jews come together, and I spoke nothing in secret. Why are you asking me these questions? Ask those who heard me. They know what I teach."

One of the temple guards struck Jesus on the face. "Is that the way to respond to the high priest?"

Jesus replied, "If I said anything wrong, you must give testimony of the wrong; but if I spoke truthfully, why do you strike me?"

Then Annas sent him to Caiaphas the high priest. The ones who arrested Jesus led him to the high priest, where the chief priests, teachers of religious law, and elders had come together.

Peter followed along behind, as did another of the disciples. They came at last to the courtyard of the high priest. The other disciple was acquainted with the high priest, so he was allowed to enter the courtyard with Jesus. Peter stood outside. The other disciple then spoke to the slave girl watching the gate, so she let Peter in also.

The guards and the household servant were standing by a charcoal fire because it was cold. Peter was standing with the guards, warming himself by the fire. He was waiting to see what was about to happen to Jesus.

In the meantime, the chief priests as well as the entire high council, or Sanhedrin, were trying to obtain testimony against Jesus, so they could put him to death. But they were not finding any. Many were giving false witness against him, but their testimonies were not consistent.

Those who did give false testimony against Jesus contradicted each other. Later, two men came forward and said, "We heard him say 'I will destroy this temple made with hands, and in three days I will build another one, made without hands.' " But even these did not get their stories straight!

Then the high priest stood up before the others and asked Jesus, "Do you not answer these charges?" Jesus kept silent; he did not answer.

Then the high priest asked him, "Are you the Christ, the Son of God? I adjure you in the name of the living God that you tell us whether you are the Christ, the Son of God."

Jesus replied, "It is as you say. I am. And you will see me, the Son of Man, seated at the right hand of God in power, and coming on the clouds of heaven."

The high priest tore his robes and said, "He has blasphemed! What further need do we have of witnesses? You have now heard the blasphemy. What is your verdict?"

"He deserves death!" And they all condemned him to death.

Then some of them began to spit at him while some slapped him in the face. They blindfolded him; then they hit him with their fists. The guards in charge of Jesus began mocking and beating him. "Prophesy, Messiah! Who hit you this time?" The guards threw all sorts of terrible insults at him. They kept hitting him as they led him away.

Peter's Denial

AS PETER WAS sitting in the courtyard, a servant girl saw him and began staring at him. She said, "You were with Jesus the Galilean, were you not?"

"No," Peter replied, "I was not."

She then said, "This man was one of Jesus' followers!"

Peter denied it again. "Woman, I neither know nor understand what you are talking about." Peter left. At that moment, a rooster crowed.

Later, out by the gate, another servant girl noticed Peter and said to those standing around, "This man was with Jesus of Nazareth. He is definitely one of those!" Another looked at Peter and said, "You must be one of them!" Peter denied it, this time with an oath. "No, I am not! I do not know the man."

About an hour later others came over to him and said, "You must be one of them; we can tell by your Galilean speech." Someone else insisted, "This must be one of Jesus' disciples because he also is a Galilean." One of the household servants of the high priest, a relative of the man whose ear Peter had cut off, asked, "Did I not see you out there in the olive grove with Jesus?" Again Peter denied it. "Man," he said, "I do not know what you are talking about." He began to curse and swear, "I do not know the man." And immediately the rooster crowed a second time.

At that moment Jesus turned and looked at Peter.

Peter remembered the words of the Lord, how he had told him, "Before the rooster crows twice you will deny me three times."

Peter went out and wept bitterly.

Questioned by the Council

When morning came, at dawn, the chief priests, elders, scribes, and the entire high council, or Sanhedrin, met again to confer together against Jesus to put him to death.

Jesus was led before this high council. They said, "Tell us if you are the Christ."

He replied, "If I tell you, you will not believe me. And if I ask you a question, you will not answer. But I, the Son of Man, will be seated at the right hand of God in power."

They all shouted, "Then are you the Son of God?" Jesus responded, "Yes, I am."

"We need no other witnesses," they shouted. "We have heard it ourselves from his own mouth." Then they bound him, and the entire council took Jesus to Pilate, who was the Roman governor.

Judas' End

WHEN JUDAS, THE one who had betrayed Jesus, realized that Jesus had been condemned to die, he was filled with remorse and took the thirty pieces of silver back to

the chief priests and elders. He said, "I have sinned, for I have betrayed an innocent man."

But they said, "What is that to us? See to that yourself!"

Judas threw the silver into the temple sanctuary, went out, and hanged himself.

The chief priests took the silver and said, "It is not lawful to put this silver in the temple treasury, since it is blood money."

They conferred together and finally decided to buy the Potter's Field, and made it into a cemetery for foreigners. That is why this field is called the Field of Blood to this day. This fulfilled the prophecy of Jeremiah,

> They took the thirty pieces of silver, the price at which he was valued by them, and purchased the potter's field, as the Lord directed.
>
> —ZECHARIAH 11:12-13

Christ before Pilate and Herod

Jesus' trial before Caiaphas had ended in the early hours of the morning.

The entire council took Jesus to the residence of the Roman governor, the Praetorium, to stand before Pilate.

His accusers did not go into the Praetorium themselves. It would have defiled them, and therefore they would not be allowed to eat the Passover. So Pilate came out to them and asked, "What accusation do you bring against this man?"

They answered, "If he were not an evildoer, we would not have delivered him to you."

So Pilate said to them, "Then take him yourselves, and judge him by your own laws."

The Jews said, "We are not permitted to put anyone to death." This fulfilled Jesus' word, telling what kind of death he would die.

They began to accuse him. "This man has been misleading our nation by telling them not to pay their taxes to Caesar and by claiming that he is Christ, a king."

Then Pilate went back into the Praetorium and called for Jesus to be brought to him. Jesus now stood before the Roman governor.

"Are you the king of the Jews?" the governor asked.

Jesus replied, "Yes, it is as you say. Is this your own question, or did others tell you about me?"

"I am not a Jew, am I?" Pilate responded. "Your own nation and the chief priests brought you here. What have you done?"

Jesus answered, "My kingdom is not of this world. If it were, my followers would fight so that I would not be handed over to the Jews. But my kingdom is not of this realm."

Pilate replied, "So you are a king?"

"You say correctly that I am a king. I was born for this, and for this purpose I came into the world—to testify to truth. Everyone who is of the truth hears my voice."

"What is truth?" Pilate asked, and then went out again to the people. He said, "I find no guilt in this man."

But they kept on insisting, saying, "He is causing riots everywhere he goes, teaching all over Judea, from Galilee even to this place."

"Oh, is he a Galilean?" Pilate replied. When he learned that Jesus belonged to Herod's jurisdiction, he sent him to Herod. Herod happened to be in Jerusalem at the time.

Herod was very glad to see Jesus because he had heard about him and had been hoping to see him perform a miracle. Herod questioned him at some length, but Jesus answered nothing.

Meanwhile, the chief priests and teachers of religious law stood there shouting their accusations.

Then Herod and his soldiers began treating Jesus with contempt and mocking him. They put a royal robe on him and sent him back to Pilate.

Herod and Pilate, who had been enemies before, became friends that day.

Pilate then called together the chief priests and other religious leaders, along with the people. Jesus came out wearing the robe, and Pilate announced his verdict: "You brought this man to me, accusing him of inciting a rebellion. I have examined him thoroughly on this charge and in your presence. I find him innocent. Herod came to the same conclusion and sent him back to us. Nothing this man has done calls for the death penalty.

"You have a custom of asking me to release someone from prison each year at Passover. So I will have Jesus flogged, and then I will release him."

The chief priests accused him harshly of many more crimes, and Jesus made no answer. Pilate asked Jesus, "Do you not hear their many charges against you? Are you not going to answer?" But Jesus did not answer a single charge. Pilate was quite amazed.

Now, it was the governor's custom to release one prisoner to the crowd each year during the Passover celebration—anyone the people requested. This year there was a notorious criminal in prison named Barabbas who had been convicted of murder, of robbery, and of taking part in an insurrection in Jerusalem against the government.

The mob began to crowd in toward Pilate, asking him to release a prisoner as usual. As the crowds gathered before Pilate's house that morning, he said to them, "Which one do you want me to release to you—Barabbas, or Jesus who is called the Messiah?" Pilate realized by now that the chief priests had arrested Jesus out of envy.

Just then, as Pilate was sitting on the judgment seat, his wife sent him this message: "Leave this innocent man alone. I had a terrible nightmare last night about him."

At this point, however, the chief priests persuaded the crowds to ask for Barabbas to be released and for Jesus to be put to death. So the governor again asked, "Which of these two do you want me to release? Should I give you the King of the Jews?"

The chief priests and elders stirred up the mob to demand the release of Barabbas. The crowd shouted back all together, "No! Not this man, but Barabbas!" Then a mighty roar rose from the crowd, and with one accord they shouted, "Kill him, and release Barabbas!"

Pilate argued with them, because he wanted to release Jesus. "But if I release Barabbas," Pilate asked them, "what should I do with Jesus, this man you call the King of the Jews, the Christ?" And they all shouted, "Crucify him! Crucify him!"

For the third time, Pilate demanded, "Why? What crime has he committed? I have found no reason to sentence him to death. I will therefore flog him and let him go."

The crowd shouted even louder for Jesus' death. "Away with him," they cried. "Away with him—crucify him!"

"You crucify him," Pilate replied. "I find him not guilty."

The Jewish leaders replied, "By our laws he should die. He called himself the Son of God."

When Pilate heard this, he was more frightened than ever. He took Jesus back into his headquarters again and asked, "Where are you from?" But Jesus gave no answer.

"You will not talk to me? Do you not realize that I have the power to release you or to crucify you?" Then Jesus said, "You would have no power over me at all unless it were given to you from above. The ones who brought me to you have the greater sin."

Then Pilate tried to release Jesus, but the Jewish leaders told him, "If you release this man, you are no friend of Caesar. Anyone who declares himself a king is a rebel against Caesar."

When they said this, Pilate went outside again and said to the people, "I am going to bring him out to you now, but understand clearly that I find him not guilty." Pilate then brought Jesus out to them again and said, "Here is the man!" Then Pilate sat down on the judgment seat on the platform that is called the Stone Pavement (in Hebrew, Gabbatha). It was about 6:00 a.m. on the day of preparation for the Passover. Pilate said to the Jews, "Behold your king!"

When they saw Jesus, the chief priests and temple guards began shouting, "Crucify! Crucify!"

Pilate responded, "Shall I crucify your king?"

"We have no king but Caesar," the chief priests shouted.

Pilate saw that he was not getting anywhere and that a riot was developing, so he sent for a basin of water and washed his hands before the crowd, saying, "I am innocent of the blood of this man. The responsibility is yours!"

All the people yelled back. "We will take responsibility for his death—we and our children!"

So their voices prevailed. Pilate, wishing to please the crowd, handed Jesus over to them to be crucified, after he had Jesus scourged.

Pilate released Barabbas for them, the man in prison for insurrection and murder. But he turned Jesus over to the Roman soldiers to have him crucified.

Some of the governor's soldiers took Jesus into the courtyard of the governor's residence, the Praetorium, and called together the entire Roman cohort around him. They stripped him and put a purple robe on him. They made a crown of long, sharp thorns and put it on his head, and they placed a reed in his right hand as a scepter.

They knelt before him in mockery, yelling, "Hail! King of the Jews!"

They hit him with their fists. They spat on him and grabbed the reed and beat him on the head with it. After mocking him, they took off the robe and put his own clothes on him.

Then they led Jesus away to be crucified.

The Crucifixion

The soldiers took Jesus, and he went out, bearing his own cross. As they led him away, they seized a passer-by named Simon, who was from Cyrene. He was coming in from the country just then, and they forced him to follow Jesus and carry his cross. (Simon is the father of Alexander and Rufus.)

Great crowds trailed along behind, including many women who were mourning and lamenting him. Jesus turned to them and said, "Daughters of Jerusalem, do not weep for me, but weep for yourselves and for your children. For the days are coming when they will say, 'Blessed are the women who are childless, the wombs that have not borne a child, and the breasts that have never nursed.' Then they will beg the mountains to fall on them and the hills to cover them. For if these things are done when the tree is green, what will happen when it is dry?"

Two others, both criminals, were led out to be executed with Jesus. Finally, they came to a place called Golgotha, which means the Place of a Skull. There they crucified him.

9:00 A.M.

It was nine in the morning when the crucifixion took place.

The soldiers gave Jesus wine mixed with myrrh, which is a bitter gall, but when he tasted it, he was unwilling to drink.

Then they nailed him to the cross and crucified him. Jesus said, "Father, forgive them, because they do not know what they are doing."

12:00 noon

Pilate posted a sign on the cross above Jesus' head, announcing the charge against him. It read: "This is Jesus the Nazarene, the King of the Jews." The place where Jesus was crucified was near the city, and the sign was written in Hebrew, Latin, and Greek so that many people could see it.

Then the chief priests said to Pilate, "Do not write 'The King of the Jews,' but 'He said I am King of the Jews.'"

Pilate responded, "What I have written, I have written."

Both criminals were crucified there with Jesus. He was on the cross in the middle, and the two others on either side. The Scripture was fulfilled that said he would be numbered with transgressors.

After the soldiers had nailed Jesus to the cross, the soldiers gambled for his clothes by casting lots to see what each man would take. They divided his outer garments among the four of them. They also took his tunic, but it was seamless, woven in one piece. So they said, "Let us not tear it but cast lots to see who wins it." This fulfilled the Scripture,

They divided my outer garments among
them, and for my clothing they cast lots.
—PSALM 22:18

The guards sat down and began to keep watch over
Jesus as he hung there.

The crowd watched. The leaders laughed and scoffed.
The people passing by shouted abuse and shook their
heads in mockery.

"Ha! You can destroy the temple and rebuild it in three
days, can you? If you are the Son of God, save yourself.
Come down from the cross!"

The chief priests, teachers of religious law, and elders mocked him. "He saved others," they scoffed, "but he cannot save himself!"

"Let this Christ, the King of Israel, come down from the cross."

"Let him save himself if he is God's chosen. Then we will believe in him!"

"He trusted in God—let God rescue him!"

"He said, 'I am the Son of God'; let him come down from the cross that we may see and believe." The soldiers also mocked Jesus. After offering him a drink of sour wine, they called out to him, "If you are the King of the Jews, save yourself!"

One of the criminals hanging beside Jesus was also hurling abuse at him, saying, "Are you not the Christ? Save yourself and us!"

The other criminal rebuked the first one and said, "Do you not even fear God? You are about to die. We are receiving what we deserve for our deeds, but this man has not done anything wrong."

Then he said, "Jesus, remember me when you come into your kingdom." Jesus answered, "I assure you, today you shall be with me in paradise."

Standing by the cross were his mother, his mother's sister, Mary the wife of Clopas, and Mary Magdalene. When he saw his mother and the disciple whom he loved standing nearby, he said to his mother, "Woman, behold your son!" Then he said to the disciple, "Behold your mother!" From that hour the disciple took her into his own home.

At noon, darkness fell over the whole land until three o'clock. The light from the sun disappeared.

3:00 P.M.

About three o'clock, Jesus cried out with a loud voice, "Eloi, Eloi, lama sabachthani?" Translated, it means, "My God, my God, why have you forsaken me?" Some of those who were standing there said, "He is calling for Elijah."

After all the things that happened, Jesus knew that everything had already been accomplished to fulfill the Scriptures, and he said, "I am thirsty." A jar of sour wine was there, so one of the guards soaked a sponge in the wine, put the sponge on a hyssop branch, and held it up to his lips so he could drink.

But the rest said, "Let us see whether Elijah will come to save him."

When he had received the sour wine, he said, "It is finished!" Then he bowed his head, and with a loud cry he said, "Father, into your hands I commit my spirit."

And with those words he breathed his last and yielded up his spirit.

And the veil of the temple was torn in two, from top to bottom. The earth shook, and rocks split apart. The tombs opened, and many bodies of saints who had fallen asleep were raised. After Christ's resurrection, they came out of the tombs and went into the holy city and appeared to many people.

The Roman officer and the soldiers were very frightened by the earthquake as well as by all that had happened and said, "Truly this was the Son of God!"

The centurion who was standing right in front of him saw the way he breathed his last, and he said, "Certainly this man was innocent." And he began praising God.

When a crowd that came to see the spectacle saw all that had happened, they returned, beating their breasts. But the friends of Jesus, including the women who had followed him from Galilee, stood at a distance watching, including Mary Magdalene, Mary (mother of James the younger and of Joseph), Salome, and Zebedee's wife, the mother of James and John. They had been followers of Jesus and had cared for him while he was in Galilee. Many other women had also come with him to Jerusalem, and they were looking on from a distance.

The Jewish leaders did not want the bodies hanging there the next day, which was the Sabbath (especially since this Sabbath was a high day), so they asked Pilate to hasten the deaths by ordering their legs to be broken so their bodies could be taken down.

So the soldiers came and broke the legs of the two men crucified with Jesus. When they came to Jesus, they saw that he was dead already, so they did not break his legs. One of the soldiers, however, pierced his side with a spear, and blood and water flowed out.

These things happened in fulfillment of the Scriptures that say,

Not a bone of him shall be broken.
—EXODUS 12:46; NUMBERS 9:12;
PSALM 34:20

and

They shall look on him whom they
pierced.
ZECHARIAH 12:10

His Burial

This all took place on the day of preparation (the day before the Sabbath).

There was a man named Joseph, a rich man from Arimathea and also a prominent member of the Jewish high council, who was a good and righteous man. (He had not consented to the council's plan and action.) He had become a disciple of Jesus, secretly, for fear of the Jews. He was waiting for the kingdom of God. This man gathered his courage and went in before Pilate and asked permission to take away the body of Jesus.

Pilate wondered if Jesus was really dead by this time. He summoned the centurion in charge and questioned him as to whether Jesus was already dead. The officer confirmed it, so Pilate issued an order to give the body to Joseph.

Joseph took Jesus' body down from the cross and took it away. Nicodemus, the man who had come to Jesus at night, also came, bringing about a hundred pounds of embalming ointment made from myrrh and aloes. Joseph also bought a long sheet of linen cloth. Together they wrapped his body in the long linen cloth with spices, which is the Jewish custom of burial. (This happened late in the afternoon.)

The place of crucifixion was near a garden, where there was a new tomb (Joseph's own), which had been carved out of rock and had never been used. It was the day of preparation, the Sabbath was about to begin, and since the tomb was close at hand, they laid Jesus there. Joseph rolled a great stone across the entrance and left.

As Jesus' body was taken away, the women from Galilee followed and saw the tomb where they placed his body. Both Mary Magdalene and the other Mary, the mother of Joseph, were sitting nearby watching. Then they went home and prepared spices and ointments to embalm him. By the time they were finished it was the Sabbath, so they rested all day, as required by the law.

His Tomb Was Sealed

The next day, the first day of the Passover, the chief priests and Pharisees went to Pilate. They told him, "We remember what that deceiver once said while he was alive: 'After three days I will rise again.' Therefore, we request that his grave be made secure until the third day. This will prevent his disciples from stealing his body and telling everyone, 'He has risen from the dead!' If that were to happen, we would be worse off than we were before."

Pilate answered, "You have a guard; secure the tomb as best you can." So they secured the tomb, and the guard set a seal on the stone.

Resurrection Morning

The morning of April 6, AD 30.

Three Women at the Tomb

After the Sabbath day, when Sunday morning was dawning, Mary (the one from Magdala) and the other Mary were on their way to look at the grave.

Suddenly, there was a great earthquake. An angel of the Lord came down from heaven. He went to the large stone and rolled it away. Then the angel sat on top of it.

His appearance was shining like lightning. His clothes were as white as snow.

The men who were guarding the tomb acted as if they were dead men; they trembled with fear.

The angel said to the women, "Do not be afraid. I know you are looking for Jesus who was nailed to the cross.

"He is not here! He was raised from death, just as he said. Come, look at the place where he lay.

"Go quickly and tell his followers: 'Jesus has been raised from death! Listen, he will go ahead of you to the land of Galilee. You will see him there.' Remember, I told you."

The women left the tomb quickly. They were afraid, yet very happy. They ran to tell Jesus' followers.

Suddenly, Jesus met them. He said, "Greetings!" They went to him, held onto his feet, and worshiped him.

Then Jesus said to them, "Do not be afraid. Go tell my brothers that they must leave for Galilee. They will see me there."

While the women were going, some of the guards went into Jerusalem. They told the most important priests everything that had happened.

The priests had a meeting with the Jewish elders. They decided to give the soldiers some money to lie.

They said to the soldiers, "Say this: 'While we were sleeping, the followers of Jesus came at night and stole his body.'

"If the governor hears about this, we will make him believe us. We will fix it; don't worry."

So, the soldiers took the money and did as they were told. This rumor has spread among Jewish people until this very day.

Very early on Sunday morning, the women came to the tomb. They brought the sweet-smelling things they had prepared.

But the women found that the rock was rolled away from the tomb.

They went in, but they didn't find the Lord Jesus' body.

While they were wondering about it, suddenly two angels stood beside them in shining clothes.

The women were frightened; they bowed their heads down to the ground. The two men said to the women, "Why are you looking here for a living person? This is a place for dead people!

"Jesus is not here. He has risen from death! Do you remember what he said in Galilee?

"Jesus said that he must be handed over to evil men, be killed on a cross, and rise from death on the third day."

Then the women remembered Jesus' words.

The women left the tomb and went to the eleven apostles and the other followers. The women told them everything which had occurred at the tomb.

The women were: Mary of Magdala, Joanna, Mary, the mother of James, and some other women. These women told the apostles everything that had happened, but the men didn't believe what the women said. It sounded crazy.

However, Peter got up and ran to the tomb. He bent down and looked in, but the only things he saw were the grave clothes. Peter went off by himself, wondering what had taken place.

Resurrection Day

Peter and John at the Empty Tomb

Then Peter and the other follower left. They went to the tomb.

Both of them were running, but the other follower outran Peter. He arrived at the tomb first.

He bent down and saw the sheets, but he did not go inside.

Then Simon Peter came, following. Peter went into the tomb. He also saw the sheets lying there.

But the handkerchief which had been on Jesus' face was not lying with the sheets. Instead, it was all alone, folded in one place.

Then the other follower, who had come to the tomb first, also went in. He saw and he believed.

(They did not yet know the Scripture which said that Jesus must rise from death.)

The two followers went back home.

Mary was standing outside the tomb, crying while she was praying. She bent down and looked into the tomb.

She saw two angels dressed in white. They were seated where Jesus' body had been lying—one at the head and one at the foot.

They asked her, "Woman, why are you crying?" She answered them, "They took my Lord away. I don't know where they put him."

After she said this, she turned around. She saw Jesus standing there, but she didn't know that it was Jesus.

Jesus said to her, "Woman, why are you crying? Who are you looking for?" Thinking that Jesus was the gardener, she said to him, "Sir, if you carried him off, tell me where you put him and I will take him away."

Jesus said to her, "Mary!" She turned and said to Jesus in Aramaic, "Rabboni!" (This word means "My Teacher!")

Jesus said to her, "Don't cling to me; I have not yet gone up to the Father. Go to your brothers and tell them this: 'I am going to my Father and your Father, to my God and your God.'"

Mary (the one from Magdala) went and told the followers, "I have seen the Lord Jesus!" She told them that he had talked with her.

Scripture References

PART 1

Matt. 26:21-29; Mark 14:18-25; Luke 22:19-30;
John 13:21-38

John 14:1-31

John 15:1-16:33

Matt. 26:30-35; Mark 14:26-31; Luke: 22:31-39

Matt. 26:36-46; Mark 14:32-42; Luke 22:40-46;
John 18:1

Matt. 26:47-56; Mark 14:43-52; Luke 22:47-53;
John 18:2-11

Matt. 26:57-68; Mark 14:53-65; Luke 22:54-55, 63-65;
John 18:12-16, 18-24

Matt. 26:69-75; Mark 14:66-72; Luke 22:56-62;
John 18:17,25-27

Matt. 27:1-2; Mark 15:1; Luke 22:66-71

Matt. 27:3-10

Matt. 27:11-31; Mark 15:2-20; Luke 23:1-25;
John 18:28-19:13,15-16

Matt. 27:32-56; Mark 15:21-41; Luke 23:26-49;
John 19:14,17-34,36-37

Matt. 27:57-61; Mark 15:42-47, 16:1; Luke 23:50-56;
John 19:38-42

Matt. 27:62-66

PART 2

Matt. 27:62-66

Matt. 28:1-15

Luke 24:1-12

John 20:3-18

Books by Gene Edwards

THE CHRONICLES OF HEAVEN

Christ Before Creation

The Beginning

The Escape

The Birth

The Triumph

The Return

THE FIRST-CENTURY DIARIES

The Silas Diary

The Titus Diary

The Timothy Diary

The Priscilla Diary

The Gaius Diary

BOOKS ON INNER HEALING

A Tale of Three Kings

The Prisoner in the Third Cell

Letters to a Devastated Christian

Exquisite Agony

Dear Lillian

AUTHOR CONTACT INFORMATION

You may contact the author at:

P.O. Box 3450

Jacksonville, FL 32206

E-mail: gene@geneedwards.com

Internet: geneedwards.com

Toll-free Telephone: 1-800-228-2665

Toll-free Fax: 1-866-252-5504